DEPRAVIKAZI

O. Spleen

RUNNING WATER PUBLICATIONS

First published in Great Britain in 2003
by Running Water Publications, PO Box 311, Brighton BN2 1XJ

Typeset by Running Water Publications
Printed and bound by Antony Rowe Limited, Eastbourne

Extracts from "Death Rattle" have previously appeared in the
June 2002 issue of Positive magazine and the May/June 2002
issue of Running Water magazine

ISBN 0 9544718 0 6

olivaspleen@yahoo.com
www.depravikazi.com
www.runningwateronline.co.uk

DEPRAVIKAZI – AN INTRODUCTION
BY
SALENA SALIVA GODDEN

I read Depravikazi from cover to cover in one sitting. Following completion my initial response was *this is important.* I was walking home along London's Brick Lane under a perfectly blue cold sky, the world leaning heavily into war, a confusion of multicoloured saris, Muslims, Sikhs, Shoreditch fashion junkies, Indian restaurants with the lure of cheap dahl, and Bollywood music pouring out of the supermarkets.

Mesmerised in my own silence and the world of Depravikazi, I was struck by this writing, its brutal honesty, fragility and beauty. This book is important – it tries to understand the domino effect we have on each other. It is important as it documents – in a style reminiscent of Hubert Selby Jr – a personal struggle to come to terms with consequence, to dismantle naiveties, to get equipped for life's cruelties. At times glaringly crude and raw, shocking then gentle; as this truth can be.

As much as it at times feels like a personal account of the familiar vulnerability of coming of age, absorbed in self-discovery and self-destruction, it is never self-pitying or overtly glorified. Our narrator shrugs like we know that that is how it is; our narrator is on our side, offering us a wry agility to examine ourselves, past and present, through the eyes of these three stories and perspectives.

When I first encountered Spleen he was a teenage boy wearing elbow-length black rubber fisting gloves and downing a concoction of snake-bite and black with whiskey. We were in Hastings town-centre toilets. After urinating, he got the fingertip of his glove caught in his fly. Having only known him a few hours, drunk and laughing at the embarrassment, there I was fiddling with his zip in order to release this entrapment. Thereafter a remarkable friendship was formed, and he was henceforth christened to a bastardisation of Saliva: Oliva.

I visited him in hospital, there when his lungs were filled, his thin legs, gaping hollow eyes, unable to swallow or inhale without wincing with pain, and coughing, terrible coughing, leading to vomiting and more coughing. He was papery and he weakly cracked jokes about his condition – his swollen heart meaning he was capable of more loving, his hallucinatory tigers. It reminded me of Blake's *Tyger Tyger, burning bright* and I was wholly affected by this burning bright thing now lying drained and grey in a hospital bed, a gaunt brown-eyed boy in elderly pyjamas, an oxygen mask and drip.

I have a very sketchy relationship with the God I was introduced to at my confirmation, but on my way home from the hospital that night I stopped in a chapel, lit a candle and prayed; for what a waste it would be if he didn't get some of this writing done. This writing that you now have here, this work that I have seen in him since the night I met him. Spleen's writing has an impeccable sense of humour in the face of the shit and the tragic – it's a gentle poke at the maggots, thus making the corpse more lively; an acute observation of the hilarity of the fragility of mortality – he always did.

As we lean heavily into these wars, then the war with HIV – because of it and in spite of it – this is important.

Salena Saliva Godden, March 2003.

DEPRAVIKAZI

AUTHOR'S NOTE

The three stories in Depravikazi: Epiphany, Death Rattle and Duke's Mound, are linked in that they are all, in some way, autobiographical. But while Death Rattle can be considered fully autobiographical, Epiphany and Duke's Mound are fictionalisations, drawing from real experiences and characters and creating an amalgam from them.

Death Rattle was initially written as catharsis after a hospitalisation, and was the starting point for what was to become Depravikazi. Epiphany and Duke's Mound were written side by side shortly afterwards.

I felt that to fictionalise Death Rattle in the same manner as the other stories would be inappropriate. The piece is much closer to an account of actual events; if I had treated it otherwise it would have lost a lot of its edge. Equally, making Epiphany and Duke's Mound more factually authentic would have complicated the characterisations – I did not wish HIV and illness to be an issue for the character Richard.

Epiphany is set in the mid-nineties when I was a teenager, whereas Duke's Mound is based on my experiences after my time in hospital. It is for this reason that the composite of the three stories is so arranged.

Oliver Speer/Spleen, October 2002.

EPIPHANY

*   *   *

DEATH RATTLE

*   *   *

DUKE'S MOUND

EPIPHANY

*   *   *

For many years, when growing all seemed fine like in a bubble; innocent, shut off and drifting, at the mercy of those more powerful; trusting and believing them. Childhood's greatest naivety is the sense that adults hold a great truth, which in time we will come to understand. BULLSHIT. We're all just as uncertain and vulnerable as the rest. "Adults" just learn to put a muzzle on the inner child and get good at faking it; growing up is about learning how to polish your exterior and suppress your desires, neutralise the burning pit of yearning that is your gut and build up walls and walls.

*   *   *

Applying pressure with her fingers, the first wave surges from her gut with a spurt …perspiration condensing on her forehead …her mouth and nasal cavity filling with bitter bile, half-digested laxatives and the distinct underlying sweetness of chocolate. Epiphany, clenching the bowl, heaves again – sour liquids and vile white froth, then a pause to gasp some air and shudder before the last dry empty retchings.

Pulling herself up onto the toilet seat, her knickers twisted at the knees, Epiphany leans towards the sink and drinks – still seated, allowing her bowels to release their warm soup – the water tasting sweet in comparison to the bile that has passed her lips. Then reaching into her pocket for the pills she has nicked from her mother …an assortment – valium, codeine, Prozac – swallowing a few and washing them down with more water. *"I KNOW WHAT YOU'RE DOING IN THERE"* – her sister banging at the door – *"let me in"* – *"…I'll be a minute."* Epiphany, lifting herself to her feet, straightens herself out in the mirror before turning to unbolt the door. *"I know what you were doing in there"* – Lettie making a gagging gesture with her fingers to her mouth …Ignoring her, Epiphany walks past into the kitchen. *"There are better ways to lose weight, you know. If you want I can take you round Dan's to score some speed"* – *"…I'm going round Richard's tonight"* – Epiphany putting a bottle of wine from her mother's wine rack under her arm. *"Tomorrow then?"* Pausing to think for a moment then smiling at her sister – *"Alright then …tomorrow."* (Epiphany had not been to 24-hour Dan's before, but was aware of his reputation.) They decide on a time as Epiphany positions her wig, straightens her skirt and unlatches the door, taking in the fresh Robertsfield air and the turned heads and looks of curiosity and disgust from the town's drab inhabitants.

At age sixteen, Epiphany had fully refined the art of pretension, mostly as a defence mechanism, but also as a form of escapism to deal with her mother's continuous onslaught of abuse. She would go out of an evening dressed in her red wig, with her mother's corset and riding crop, to confuse the goth kids and skaters who hung around the town centre with stories of how she beat little boys into submission. Epiphany thought most of the kids in the town were superficial small-minded arseholes anyway. She didn't intend to even try to get into their headspace, instead employing tactics of seduction and confusion, pushing her tits up in her corset so they appeared round and plumped. She knew that boys fell for her striking looks, so when they made a pass at her she could push them away with a look of disgust and – *"I wouldn't fuck you if you were the last prick around, baby."*

Richard, however, was a good friend to her – a real friend, and someone to look forward to when the holidays came and she had to leave her school friends to return to the dead-end town of her birth. She and Richard lived in the same street, and had played together when she was five and he was only four, before her mother had sent her to The Sacred Heart Catholic School For Girls. Now it was the summer holidays again and the only safe haven from her family was Richard's house.

Checking her reflection in the glass of the door, Epiphany rings the bell. She hears some movement in the hall, and stands to one side as the door is opened. *"Hello"* – Richard's mother's greeting, as ever, robust and warm – *"come on in, how are you? How's school been?"* – *"...Fine, thank you"* – Epiphany softening her usual abrasive edge. She had, in fact, been suspended twice in the last year of school, once for truancy and the second time because she'd been caught masturbating, using a small plaster statue of the Virgin Mary as a dildo. But she decides to leave out this information, instead smiling with a coy innocence at the foot of the stairs that lead to Richard's room. *"Is Richard in?" – "Yes, I think he's being a teenager in his room, do go on up"* – Richard's mother smiling another warm smile as Epiphany climbs the stairs.

The crushing weight of puberty had descended on Richard two summers earlier, when, on holiday with his parents, he had gone into the toilet and masturbated for two hours solid, coming again and again until his penis was red raw and bloated like a rugby ball. The swelling went down after an agonising couple of days, in which any kind of chafing brought on by walking or activity of any description caused him to moan in pain – he'd had to pretend he was sick so as to avoid any family outings.

Opening the door, Epiphany imagines she can feel the room inhale, reviving itself of its tomb-like humidity. As with the bedrooms of many teenage boys, Richard's room smells of a combination of dried semen and rancid bong-water; the only person impervious to the smell being Richard's mother, who, blissfully unaware of Richard's habits, rarely enters his bedroom, preferring instead to remain naive to the practices of teenage boys. Once guests have become accustomed to this odour, they are struck by the magnificent state of the place – every inch of wall a collage of things Richard has found interesting; his oil paintings; pictures of circus freaks, toys and flowers glued to the wall in various stages of decomposition, lit up by strings of fairy lights that illuminate the wisps of bong smoke. The ceiling too is covered, every object of some personal value or relevance to Richard; surfaces adorned with fine artefacts, African sculptures indiscriminately placed among misted pint glasses of three-day urine. Epiphany, looking around at how the room has evolved since her last visit, jumps as Richard emerges heavy-lidded from the clutter, his long arms outstretched to embrace her – *"Pifff! I haven't seen you in ages!"* With a wasted grin he engulfs her in his ganglyness and she hugs him back. *"I missed you. What have you been up to?"* Epiphany's stomach rumbling, its tender lining struggling to digest the chemical concoction as she hands him the wine bottle – *"Oh... school shit, my mother being a freak as usual"* – clearing a space to sit – *"...she's been saying that my father was an arsehole and that I was a mistake and everything"* – yawning with contempt – *"...just the usual shit ...how about you?"* Richard looking about the floor for a corkscrew – *"Ooh... I thought you'd be down, so I got some acid and..."* – swallowing nervously, his eyes still scanning the rubble of the floor – *"I've been doing some really fucked-up shit that I can't tell anyone about."* Epiphany looks up at his face to see his head down, eyes nervously scanning the floor as if avoiding eye contact. *"...What is it, heroin?"* – *"No, nothing like that ...I can't tell you"* – *"You can't just say something like that and then not tell me what it is you're talking about."* Richard, producing a corkscrew from under his battered armchair, smiling a half smile – *"Well then, I'll tell you later."*

Opening the bottle of wine he pours it into a mug, which they share as they talk about school. Richard sounding woeful as he talks of how he will be glad to get out of his shithole of a school; that the other kids think of him as a freak (rarely a day goes by that he doesn't find great globs of phlegm hanging from his school shirt), and how, in his school, they aren't encouraged to have any prospects beyond working on a factory production line or the civil service or accountancy, and he can't do maths or spell properly. Instead Richard is looking forward to going on the dole so he can paint and live as a recluse. That or suicide, and, contrary to the belief of many, suicide is not an easy option, so, not wanting his attempts to look like pathetic cries for help, he has decided instead to refrain from the contemplation until he musters the guts to do it properly. Epiphany, however, has visions way beyond apathetic Robertsfield. She talks of how a major art critic came to her school and wanted to buy one of her pieces, but she wouldn't sell as his offer was too low. But when she gets out of school she will go to London and university and her work will be acclaimed and everyone will want a piece of her and Richard should come too. But he is unsure whether anyone will have him; speaking heavy-heartedly of how he resents the education system as it only ever makes him feel inadequate. Feeling instead that the most important lessons life has taught him he has learned outside school – *"School is just a place where they condition people to feel disempowered so that they'll be of little trouble in the future."*

Epiphany, sensing a subtext to his downheartedness, tells him to stop being such a miserable cunt and asks him what's wrong – *"What was the fucked-up shit you were saying you've been up to?"* Richard becoming quite flushed, swallowing deeply and attempting a carefree air as he speaks – *"…I've been meeting people…in toilets"* – his voice wavering but trying to sound confident – *"we're not having sex or anything"* – half regretting what he is saying as the words come out, so terrified of what the response may be – *"just wanking …and oral sex, but that makes me gag."* Epiphany looking up at him, his eyes again averted – *"Are you gay?"* – *"NO!"* – his reply an automatic defence mechanism – *"…well, perhaps a bit, but I'm not a faggot, like those cunts at school say I am; I've just got a high sex drive. But the men I've been with are disgusting …like my dad's age, and I don't know why I keep doing it"* – Richard sighing as he feels a great weight lift from him. Though mildly repulsed at the thought that Richard would allow filthy middle-aged randoms to dominate and abuse him when she, his best friend, would be quite happy and capable of dominating and abusing him herself, Epiphany smiles piously and embraces his skinny frame – *"…I'd fuck you,*

9

you're a handsome boy." Richard taking a deep breath and pausing in thought, then blinking back a tear and smiling wickedly – *"Shall we do the acid?"*

*   *   *

Over an hour has passed since they swallowed the Red Dragon blotters; Richard pulling another bong and cursing the crusty that burned him as he exhales. Then Epiphany, noticing a tingling sensation at the back of her mind and a shifting geometry beyond her field of vision – *"I'm starting to come up"* – her voice buoyant with anticipation. *"I'm not"* – Richard's response pessimistic. *"No, look"* – Epiphany moving her arms fluidly in front of Richard's face, her movements seeming to emit a pattern of traces radiating in a kaleidoscope. *"…Fuck yeah!"* – Richard's face stretching to a grin and turning to look around the room. He sees that every object, from the paintings on the wall, the dusty ribbons and baubles that hang from the beams of the ceiling, down to the precious litter strewn across the floor, seems to be radiant with life. *"…We should go for a walk – I don't want to stay in the house with my parents downstairs."* Giggling, they sneak down the stairs and past the living room, where Richard's parents are watching TV – *"Are you off out?"* – the voice of Richard's dad, with an alien authority. *"Yes …for a while"* – Richard trying to sound serious, then Epiphany bursting into floods of laughter and Richard following, creasing up, as they run down the hallway and out into the evening.

*   *   *

The dusk, now emanating purple-pink they trip exquisite, encased in bubble, senses wired. At times abstraction fleck across the conscious mind to babble incoherence and laugh till tears roll down. At moments; complete unity, each other, of sky and endless space, the great globe beneath their feet, the gravity of flesh, this human receptor in overdrive, experience, absorbing the very essence. Sometimes entire fabric of existence and time dilate with broken glimpses of lucidity; complete realisation. To turn to face the other and absorbed in blackness of the pupil – *"…You look fuuucked"* – then laugh again and touching hand and flesh, feel membrane rubberised with luminescence; pink and green. The skin of cheek is too like rubber – pulling – laughing – pulling, marshmallow tread of grass underfoot and fall and laugh and disappear for a brief eternity among the infinite fractals of the moss and part the grass's leaves like giants who hear insects whisper in its soil. Then stabilise to stabilise to rise to feet and feel a balance, stabilise a level of ambiguity and onwards, keeping to the gravel paths that top the marvelled crescent of the hill she place her wig on Richard's head and laugh as he run fingers through and pout his lips – a passing kid shouts – *"Faggot"* – Richard retract into himself, the word still ringing in his head, the – FAGGOT – word – FAGGOT – still – FAGGOT – ringing – FAGGOT – ringing – FAGGOT – ringing. Epiphany not hearing what kid said but turn, see Richard gone and wig lay in the path cries – *"Richard …RICHAAARD"* – and hear moan from bushes and – *"Do you think I'm a fag?"* – as Richard grapple with his mind to rid him of the word so as to deftly slip the grasp of certain knowledge, diffuse the onslaught of his brain, his dick, his urges, tired flesh unable to fight this masturbatory war so long sustained, giving in to himself with the decision that he would sleep with Epiphany and then the truth be known for sure. And she calm him and stroke his hair and touch her warmth to him and he feel her kindness melting where he's cold – *"Who cares if you're a fag, you are a good person, Richard, you are a good person."*

From then, the hours melt and time seems too soon as Epiphany reaches her door. They kiss goodbye, and, watching his walk to the distance, she giggles as he appears smaller and smaller until in a land for dolls. They have long passed their peak and – fried though they are – they find it possible to comprehend sleep after seeing the morning's first glow to the east. Epiphany creeping up the stair and finding her place to bed in darkness. Then attempting to focus on the repetitive neon patterns of the dark, Aztec dogs that turn to serpents who eat themselves and are reborn. The seam between this state and asleep, barely detectable and blurring more so as …Epiphany …gently …slips …through.

*   *   *

She did not know how long she'd been sleeping, or if she'd been sleeping at all. Unsure, as she lay, that she was even awake, but half-aware of music from somewhere. The neon patterns have subsided, but her mind is still emitting a glow of comfort, heavy with the disorientation of her state of slumber …and then there is the music, slowly seeping into her consciousness, the sweet melodic strains of an overture, seeming to emanate from somewhere below. *'Am I in my mother's house?'*

Teetering between a state of wake and dream, Epiphany starts to piece together in her mind a picture of herself, the previous night, the room in which she lay, where she came from and how she now found herself to be where she was. It *is* her mother's music she can hear: the opening piece of an opera by Wagner – the music gently undulating beneath her bed.

Epiphany's mother had spent the best part of the first thirty years of her life bulimic. Three of these years were spent studying opera music until she became inadvertently pregnant with Epiphany's elder half-sister Violetta (Lettie), named after Verdi's doomed heroine. It was Epiphany's father who had named *her*. He, like his daughter, was an artist, but he had died when she was too young to remember him beyond a vague outline of memory; the accompanying nostalgic emotion when she looked at the photographs that her mother did not know she had kept.

Now an embittered and delusional prima donna, earning her living as a voice trainer, Epiphany's mother rarely talked of her husband outside one of her dramatic and all too regular outbursts. Epiphany was uncertain why he had wanted to commit suicide and leave his daughter, and any attempt by her to delve deeper into the matter with her mother was greeted with melodramatic distress, much wailing and shouting, and an insistence that the subject never be broached.

Still nestling, eyes closed beneath the covers, Epiphany thinks she can hear the door open – the music sounding clearer. She is aware of a presence in the room, a rummaging and scuffling of feet with impatient breaths; the curtains are swept open, flooding the room with summer sun – Epiphany covering her face with her bed covers. It is her mother in the room; she is preparing herself for her aria.

"And where were you last night?" Epiphany remaining motionless beneath the covers until her mother pulls them back, causing Epiphany to cover her eyes with her arm as her pupils adjust to the light – *"…Richard's"* – her voice weak and hoarse. *"Don't think I don't know what you're up to, I'm not stupid"* – Epiphany's mother looming over the bed, her dyed-black meringue of hair silhouetted against the window – *"you're on drugs, aren't you? …Out until god knows what hour; is this how you behave at school?"* Epiphany remaining silent and expressionless. *"That Richard's a bad influence on you …taking drugs …STEALING MY THINGS"* – holding the corset aloft, her voice now reaching falsetto as the music erupts

13

below – *"you rummage through my private life with no regard to how I feel."* Epiphany slumping lower in the bed – *"I was just borrowing..."* – *"DO YOU THINK I WANT IT BACK NOW YOU'VE SOILED IT!?"* – Epiphany's mother falling dramatically to the bed as her cadenza approaches its finale. Then holding her hands out to Epiphany in the pose of a martyr – *"Look at my hands, they're trembling ...see what you do to me ...how you make me feel. I never used to shake like this ...it was your father, fucking off ...leaving me with all the responsibility ...he was selfish, just like you ...selfish, self-absorbed..."* – *"I don't need to hear this"* – Epiphany covering her face with a pillow. *"...SELFISH, SELF-ABSORBED, CHILDISH ...I need a cigarette ...and a drink ...SEE WHAT YOU DO, YOU DRIVE ME TO DRINK!!"* There is a pause as Epiphany's mother, rising to her feet, stands with her head held high as if awaiting her encore. Epiphany, numbed to the performance, remains silent. Producing an indignant grunt, her mother turns in a flurry of silk and exits stage left, leaving Epiphany to sink back beneath the covers, where she huddles foetal, swallowing back the taste of salt and tears.

*   *   *

"Who is it?" – comes the voice, and Lettie, recognising Dan's swagger silhouetted on the frosted glass – *"...It's Lettie."* Dan unlocking the door – *"Hello ladies, do come on in. Excuse the mess."* As Violetta and Epiphany kick their way through the beer cans, half-eaten kebabs and pizza boxes to the sofa, where Keith (Dan's best mate) is pulling a double-barrelled bong. *"...This is my sister, Piff."* Epiphany smiling coyly in the presence of these older (albeit somewhat rough-looking) boys; the lads admiring Epiphany's cleavage – *"Piff! What kind of name's that?"* Epiphany attempting to react to Dan's comment with aloof disdain, but instead finding herself becoming embarrassingly girlie, finding Dan and Keith

14

strangely desirable and herself somewhat turned on by them, yet at the same time mildly repulsed; and finding this emotion to be in itself erotic. *"…It's short for Epiphany."* Dan screwing his face up and laughing through his nose – *"Your mum must've been off her head when she had you both."* And Keith echoing the sentiment with a grunt as he expels his smoke.

"…We were just wondering if you had any speed to sell?" Dan lifting his scales and producing a wooden box from underneath – *"…As it happens, ladies, I do"* – producing five plastic sealy-bags from the box – *"…five grams quality base-paste, going at a tenner a gram"* – *"Just one will do"* – Epiphany handing him a tenner. *"You might want to cut it with glucose or somefing – that shit'll make your gums bleed …I don't touch it anymore myself; I'd rather do a line of charlie any day."* Epiphany looks at the clear plastic baggie – the amphetamine inside is yellow in colour and feels squishy through the bag. She holds it up to her nose and smells it – a pungent chemical smell, like ammonia or bad urine. *"So, what are you girls up to?"* – Dan's grin stretching from ear to ear. *"Oh… we're just down for the holidays. Piff's back from school."* Dan raising his eyebrows in interest – *"Oh yeah? …A schoolgirl! What school?"* Epiphany reacting in a cool and disinterested manner – *"Sacred Heart, I'm starting my A-levels…"* – *"A catholic girl! I bet you're all sexually frustrated, locked up in there with each uvva."* Epiphany smiling with some unease as Keith pisses himself laughing. *"Still, I bet you get a lot of hot girl-on-girl action, nowotImean?"* Keith choking on his beer, the beer coming out of his nose. Lettie cuts in – *"We'd better be off now. Thanks for sorting us out"* – *"…Sure ladies, anytime."* And Keith, unmoved from his spot on the sofa – *"…Yeah, we'll sort you out anytime – HAHAHAHAHA…"* – the sound of Keith's laughter still audible even after the door is closed behind them.

It is getting dark as Epiphany reaches the road where she and Richard live. The summer smells good, as if buzzing with the energy of excitement and possibility. It is in these rare moments that Epiphany acknowledges that she is young, and that life is hers to grab head on. The nostalgia of the buildings and streets in which she spent the first five years of her life are making her feel slightly melancholy, but this is overridden by the good energy she is feeling – the realisation that she will only be back for a short while, and will soon leave these streets, her mother, and the petty-minded people of Robertsfield – *'Life has got great things in store for me. It's just a shame that Richard can't seem to see beyond this shithole.'*

She shouts up to the window on the third floor, where he is sitting, legs dangling out, drinking a bottle of wine, the pulsating drone of The Velvet Underground audible from where Epiphany stands below. *"I'LL JUST GET MY KEYS"* – Richard disappearing into the candlelit darkness of his room, then re-emerging to almost lose his balance as he tosses the keys over the cars to where she stands.

Letting herself in and up the stairs she kisses Richard on the cheek, and, taking the bottle of wine from his hand, joins him on the window ledge. Richard passing her a cushion to perch on – *"How were you after the acid the other night?"* Epiphany taking a big swig from the wine – *"I couldn't sleep properly. I don't know how long I was up for."* Richard smiling as he takcs back the wine – *"Tell me about it! I was up all night masturbating …it's fucking weird watching yourself have a wank while you're tripping."* Epiphany raising an eyebrow with a smile – *"What? You were wanking in front of the mirror! …You must be a poof."* Richard becoming defensive at the accusation, blushing and wracking his brain for a valid justification – *"Don't you think it's interesting to be aware of yourself on that level? Flesh can seem so alien when you're tripping …the idea of sex and human lust is so fucking absurd! …It's just interesting sometimes to get a good look at yourself"* – *"What?! …Having a wank?!"* Richard still struggling to explain himself – *"Errr …it's about fully confronting your carnal side."* Epiphany grinning in disbelief – *"Yeah right, you just get off on your own naked body …YA POOF!!"* And Richard joking her back, his nudge almost knocking her off the windowsill – *"Fuck you! I'd shag a girl any day!"* Epiphany, looking at him knowingly and snatching back the wine – *"Hey Bitchard! …I got us some speed from Dan's. Do you have anything to cut it with, like glucose or something?"* – *"What do you think I am? A fucking chemist? Lemme see…"* – he goes downstairs, emerging moments later with a bag of icing sugar – *"…do you think this'll do?"* Epiphany looking doubtful – *"It'll probably go all gloopy"* – then remembering there are still some pills nicked from her mother at the bottom of her pocket – *"I know what'll work."* Richard, taking his mirror from the wall, clears a space on the floor so it can lay flat. Epiphany crushes the pills with a cash card against the mirror then, producing the sealy-bag and mixing an amount in with the crushed powder – *"It seems to be absorbing the stickiness. Do you reckon you could snort that?"* – *"…I'll certainly give it a try"* – rolling up a five pound note – *"you go first."*

As the bitter mixture hits the back of Epiphany's nasal cavity, it stays there a while suspended, caustic, before another snort encourages it to take the slide down the back of her gullet. Richard follows soon after, noticing the strong underlying rancidness to the taste, as yellow in flavour as the substance had first appeared. Finding it is taking time to kick in and heavy with anticipation, they imbibe more cheap wine and share a bong, letting the conversation take its natural course. *"Does your mother have any idea of the shit you get up to in here?"* – *"No!"* – Richard's reaction an outburst, as a memory pops into his head – *"…I love my mum – she can be so blissfully naive. At first I assumed they knew about everything I got up to but chose to turn a blind eye …and then one day last year I came back from school to find my bong was moved and the mix dish had been washed up …she said she wanted a talk and I thought 'oh fuck …drugs talk, what am I going to say?' …You won't believe what she said…"* Epiphany staring intently – *"Go on…"* – *"She said 'I know that you smoke – it would be hypocritical for me to say that you shouldn't. I'm just glad that you use a wet ashtray as it is a fire hazard'!? …She had assumed that I had bought an antique pipe and filled it with water to use as an ashtray so I wouldn't set the house on fire! …Fucked-up logic"* – *"…Jesus! My mum can practically smell if I've been doing anything she wouldn't approve of …which is pretty much everything …I wish I had a mum like yours."* Richard feeling the first surges of energy propel his emotions, and so reacting with enthusiasm – *"Yeah, she's cool … it sometimes worries me to think how upset she might be if she really knew the things I did"* – taking the rolled-up five pound note from Epiphany's hand; and feeling a tingling in his arms and back with mild palpitations as his heartbeat quickens, Richard proceeds to follow her in the snorting of another line.

One bottle of wine is finished; Richard reaching into the cardboard box to take out another – *"This shit costs £1.50 a bottle. The bloke two doors down gets it in from France by the vanload …that's one thing my parents can do: drink. They're probably too pissed to know what goes on up here"* – uncorking the bottle of wine; the wine and speed and conversation continuing to flow, propelled to greater and greater heights, each of them paying far more attention to what they have to say next than in listening to the other – *"...this is what life is about!"* – Richard grinning, eyes wide, his jaw clenching into the flesh on the inside of his cheek – *"...have you got any chewing gum?"* Epiphany rummaging in her pocket – *"I don't think so..."* Richard not registering her reply; instead enthusing about the feeling whilst chewing dead skin from his lip and gnawing again at his cheek – *"Life is about sensation ...how do we know we're alive if we don't feel?"* Epiphany emptying one of Richard's clouded pint glasses out of the window, pouring the urine slowly so it trickles down the tiles and into the gutter and drainpipe, and then promptly positioning herself so she can fill the glass again – *"Do you like a bit of pain then?"* – Epiphany's grin manic as she squats, crouching to release the waters of her bladder. *"I reckon I am more masochistically inclined than sadistic"* – Richard remembering something, the thought urgently erupting to the forefront of his mind – *"...my mother would often quote that biblical verse, 'do unto others as you would have them do to you' ...or whatever it is. But there's plenty of shit I wouldn't mind having done to me that I wouldn't dream of doing to anyone else."* Epiphany placing the pint glass to the side before reaching for the speed bag, rubbing some neat on her gums and wincing with the chemical bitterness – *"...What kind of shit?"* – passing the bag to Richard and reaching for the wine bottle; Richard taking the bag and dabbing an amount with his fingertip – *"...Oh, nothing in particular ...nothing I'd want to tell anyone about anyway ...I just sometimes get weird urges, fantasies about abuse scenarios ...things being done to me against my will"* – feeling a shiver down his spine with the realisation that he is saying things out loud that he's hardly consciously admitted to himself yet – *"...it makes me sick that I think such things ...I guess I don't like myself if I think about it too much."* Epiphany lighting a cigarette – *"Everyone gets like that though ...sometimes I look at my body and I wish I had more control over it ...sometimes I just want to fill myself with the most useless unhealthy crap – cheap cakes and sweets; the kind of shit I know I shouldn't be eating ...so I feel guilty and make myself sick, and for that time I feel like my body is mine and I'm in control ...I know I'm fucked up, but at least that awareness is something to hold on to..."* – Taking a deep breath, recoiling from her speech, surprised at how her thoughts seem to be spat forth from somewhere deep inside, the verbalisation of the emotions she has long felt. *"Burn me with your cigarette"* – Richard lifting up the sleeve of his shirt to present his upper arm. Epiphany surprised at first, and Richard acknowledging her surprise, so repeating himself with greater certainty – *"...burn me with your cigarette!"* Epiphany warming to the idea, holding the butt of her cigarette between thumb and forefinger and pulling taut the flesh of his upper arm as if it were a canvas, positioning the tool of her art carefully to slowly extinguish the embers into his soft tissue; Richard clenching his teeth – his jaw locking. The pain is such that the first impulse is to withdraw, but with the butt now fully immersed in his arm, the sensation becomes heightened; exhilarating, radiating out from the blackened circle with a glow. Richard letting out a sigh and laying back, tingling from the sensation; the comfort he is feeling in acknowledging his crapulence and being able to share in this experience with someone to whom he feels very close. *"Now you do me"* – her voice wavering slightly. Richard picking up the butt and re-lighting it, looking her in the eye to know for sure that it's what she wants before bringing the ember down onto her skin; Epiphany emitting a groan of acute pain, slowly subsiding into an almost orgasmic sigh as a rush of sensation passes through her. Then laying back in Richard's arms – *"...we should have sex ...I mean just as friends ...to see what it's like"* – looking up at him, awaiting his response; Richard blushing and feeling a bit nervous – *"...Yeah ...I've been wanting to, if not just to help sort out this sexuality shit*

20

in my head" – "…Well let's do it then …it's just fucking" – Epiphany loosening his belt. *"…I'm not sure how easy it will be to get hard, what with the speed and all"* – Richard reaching into his pants and finding himself semi-hard, probably mostly due to the absurdity of the situation, remembering how in primary school he would get erections if he was made to stand up in class or assembly, having to awkwardly conceal himself with a hymn-book or textbook. Taking it out, Epiphany starts sucking, Richard putting his head back and closing his eyes to let the sensations take over. For a while he is lost, then, feeling that it would be polite to participate more, he reaches towards her, touches her breast and kisses her; her skin feels soft and delicate, Richard finding the experience more sensual than sexual, enjoying kissing her, his close friend, but feeling somewhat repelled by her softness, her femininity, fully aware of her aesthetic beauty, though finding that beauty inspires no lust in him. Epiphany taking his hand and placing it between her legs, Richard noticing the folds and creases of skin, the moisture, the hair, wanting to pull his hand away but Epiphany encouraging his fingers to enter, Richard contemplating going down on her, then picturing her pink folds and the smell, and feeling like he's out of his depth – *'I'll just fuck her then, it'll be over in a bit'* – Richard mounting and fumbling and Epiphany guiding him and coaxing and encouraging him with moans of delight; enjoying exerting her control, leading Richard into this uncharted territory and finding pleasure in the notion that she's corrupting him. *'I can thrust and stay erect …surely that will be enough'* – Richard slotting into a rhythm with his pumping occasionally increasing in pace, Epiphany's gasps breathless, her fingers clawing into Richard's back, Richard thrusting into her, his thrusts becoming trance-like, robotic, becoming Zen with it, clearing his mind and becoming unaware of the passing of time or what he is doing …then breaking back to consciousness again and speeding up in the hope it will soon be over, noticing her body trembling and gasps quicken – *"Oh yeah ...ohhhhh"* – as she claws deeper into his back and wraps her legs around him, and Richard faking some groans of pleasure before withdrawing his cock and turning to his armchair to retrieve some pictures collected from sports pages and men's underwear catalogues, so reaching his climax beating furiously with his fist, his semi-flaccid speed penis emptying itself into a milky puddle on the floor; and Richard sinking back into his inadequacy, then consoling himself with the thought – *'I managed to sustain an erection ...I can't be completely queer.'* And Epiphany breaking through his introverted contemplation with – *"HAHAHA ...you are sooo a poof"* – as she pisses herself at Richard's collection of pictures, and they lay back in each other's arms and sweat, bemused at how the time just seems to slip from underneath them, and still slipping they drink and smoke to the acceptance of Richard's queerness, until the morning light penetrates their well-worn conversation, so with a desperate sinking feeling they darken the room, and, cocooned from the summer sun, they eventually muster a few strung-out scraps of sleep, interspersed with waves of paranoia and psychosis.

*   *   *

It is mid-afternoon as Epiphany crosses the street to her home, the summer sun hurting her eyes and head. They had licked out the last of the speed an hour earlier, as Richard had to do some work for his dad; Epiphany starting to feel another wave of energy, though the chasm of chemical despair she feels inside is overwhelming. In a sense she's enjoying this hollow feeling as a reaffirmation of her inadequacy; she hasn't eaten at all either, so that is something to feel good about.

Unlocking the door she listens, relieved to hear that her mother isn't around. Then walking into the kitchen to open the fridge and taking out a bottle of mineral water and a small yoghurt (just to line her stomach), and, noticing an opened bottle of wine, she puts it under her arm and proceeds to her room. She had wanted to go to Dan's later to get some more speed, but is feeling too paranoid to face anyone she doesn't know that well – *'Some wine will help.'*

After a couple of mouthfuls of yoghurt (which she had to wash down with water as the consistency made her gag) she then proceeds with the wine, observing there is the best part of two-thirds of a bottle left. The wine seems to sit better on her stomach, and with each sip some of the energy and sensations of the previous night seem to be coming back to her; only now the sensations are one day more ingrained, so adding another layer to her wastedness. Drawing the curtains of her room and looking for some music – wanting something chilled, but unable to decide between Miles Davis or Tricky. Then eventually settling with Miles, she lies back in her darkness, and, lighting a cigarette, laughs at the memories of the previous night through the fogged cloud of her brain, wondering how Richard is doing – *'This'll be a summer we'll remember.'*

*   *   *

"I see the girl's come back for some more billy, is it? …C'mon in" – as Dan, eyes wired, pauses to dislodge something glutinous from his nasal cavity – *"…spect you might like a taste of cock – hrrmph – coke an' all?"* – *"Yeah… why not"* – Epiphany stumbling through the doorway as Keith, on the sofa, snorting back his laughter (also lodged somewhere at the back of his nose), cuts the white powder; then passing her the mirror and Epiphany falling back into the sofa, almost spilling it. *"Oi! Watch it, girl!"* And reaching for the card to straighten out the line, she takes half of another with it, then, with the rolled up twenty, proceeds to snort them both, making it look like an accident. *"The girl's got some fuckin cheek,*

nowotImean?" And Epiphany grinning eyes-wide as the sensation creeps numbingly from her nose to her tongue to her whole head until she is fully nestled in a buzzing comfort, devoid of the chemical bitterness of the previous night. Keith is pinching ash from the ash tray, which he sprinkles over some holes in a crumpled beer can; Dan passes her a bottle of Jack Daniels, she takes a large swig, then retching into her mouth, swallows it back and asks for water; Dan respectfully obliging with an unwashed mug under the cold tap, Keith chipping off a small white piece of rock and placing it on the ash then asking Dan if they should let her have a taste and Epiphany – *"I'll try anything."* Dan instructing her to breathe out fully first then keep it in for as long as possible, and holding the flame a few centimetres above so the heat is sucked in enough to ignite the rock; Epiphany expecting it to make her cough but finding it to be more like inhaling a gas than smoke and noticing a change in atmosphere as she holds the vapour in and Dan taking the can and sorting himself one and Epiphany's heart rate increasing and Dan holding his smoke in, then shifting legs-splayed to her side and Epiphany experiencing rushes of heightened sexual-chemical energy as Dan reaches smoothly up her thigh and Epiphany reaching over to the bulge in his jeans and unable to control a burst of laughter at its apparent (lack of) size and Dan – *"What the fuck's wrong wiv you girl?"* And Keith looking on and grinning and Dan telling him to – *"go fuck off somewhere, you can get some afterwards, I aint a fuckin poof!"* And Keith dabbing himself some coke before reluctantly exiting to the other room and blasting on some garage and Dan shouting at him to – *"TURN THAT FUCKIN SHIT DOWN!"* – then lowering his jeans and pants, his veined toadstool of a cock springing to attention and sprinkling a little coke on the end and raising an eyebrow to Epiphany – *"suck it."* And Epiphany laughing and dispassionately sucking the end and Dan forcing her head

24

onto it and Epiphany gagging on it and, feeling the bile rise from her gut, pushing him away with – *"Fuck off!"* And Dan sitting back down next to her and reaching over to grope a tit and Epiphany taken by another wave of sensation, perspiring, her heartbeat rising as she slumps lower in the sofa and parts her legs and Dan sliding his hand under the elastic of her knickers, through a forest of bush to the warm folds of her snatch and Epiphany wriggling ecstatic as the bodily sensations of flesh on flesh mingle with the chemicals in her brain to erupt in electric ripples across her skin, then breaking out of the subtlety of the experience as Dan clumsily mounts her and pushes it in; Epiphany unaware as he thrusts what she is feeling, unable to feel the cock inside her but sure it must be there, unable to fully comprehend where she is or what she is doing but feeling dirty, feeling abused and finding solace in that feeling until she is lost in the slap slap slap of Dan's flesh against hers and as the slapping speeds up and eventually stops she is aware of Dan moving away and some shouting through the music of the other room; though unable to move still laying legs-splayed, wrapped in the sordid comfort of her degradation and only mildly conscious of some fumbling by her open legs and a hand upon her tit before she is parted by an altogether larger cock.

*   *   *

In Richard's dream he is imprisoned within four high stone walls on a hill's incline by the sea. Uncertain as to the exact reason for his imprisonment he feels sure that the "crime" he has committed is only a crime in the eyes of an unjust law.

The hours seem to drag in the cold solitude of his incarceration, and it seems an eternity before the glowing orange of the sun dips behind the walls and night draws in. With the coming of night (the moon bright in the sky) also comes the tide, seeping in through the cracks between the stones. At first Richard is frightened that he might drown, but as the water reaches his feet he finds it is warm and welcoming, and so submerges himself naked in its warmth.

Swimming in the warm sea confines of his roofless cell, he comes across a small and golden squid. They instantly develop a bond unlike anything Richard has experienced. He feels certain it is love and – though the squid cannot communicate its feelings verbally to Richard – as they frolic he is sure that what they are experiencing is mutual. Time just slips away, and both Richard and the squid are deeply saddened when the first glow of the morning sun creeps over the horizon and with it comes the lowering tide and the squid's departure.

The bitter pill of his incarceration seems so much more digestible with the thought that, come night-time, the tide will rise again and Richard will see his beautiful squid. As the days and nights pass and their bond develops, Richard and the squid achieve orgasm by rubbing their bodies together. The "sex" they engage in (however strange it may appear to an outsider) seems the most perfect, pure and innocent act to Richard and the squid – utterly devoid of any feelings of sin or guilt or shame. Wrapped in the joy of these moments Richard is sure he has never felt so whole.

After what is probably a couple of months (really just seconds in the blurred and rushing timescale of his dream), Richard is pardoned by the authorities, who are most apologetic at the injustice of their laws. They ask Richard if there is anything they can give him to compensate him for his hardship. Richard asks only that he can have a saltwater pool fitted, so he can live in peace with his beloved squid. His wish is granted and, in light of their heroic tale of love in the face of adversity – a love that crosses the great chasm between man and squid – they are asked to appear on the TV show "This Morning" with Richard and Judy.

Cut to: Richard on the "This Morning" couch, the golden squid in a tank by his side. Richard Madeley (the presenter) starts his introduction – *"Now, it's a lovely story we have up next. It's only recently that man-squid relationships have been acknowledged in our society, but here we have an unparalleled love story that crosses the boundaries of sea and land..."* A disembodied voice cuts in – *"RICHAAARD!"* Richard Madeley swivelling in his seat and looking around him; Judy pointing – *"His name's Richard too."* Richard starting to acknowledge that this is all a dream – *"I think the voice is coming from outside."* And again – *"RIIICHAAAARD!!"* He awakens with a start...

"Let me in, I've been out here for ages" – Epiphany looking dishevelled on the street beneath his window. *"One second..."* – looking around for his keys, still blurry-headed from his deep sleep. Then tossing his keys down and noticing the time – 6:34am; Richard sinks beneath his covers with a groan. Epiphany letting herself in and up the stairs, then clawing the bed covers off Richard and laughing and snorting and speaking all at once – *"Ohhhjeezus amIfucked."* And Richard taking back the covers – *"You disturbed my beautiful dream."* And Epiphany – *"HelpleeeasetoofuckedthepillIneedthemorningafter"* – expelling all her air as she speaks, then filling her lungs all at once with a – *"...UUUUGHHHHH!"* And Richard sitting up and asking if she's okay, and Epiphany remembering to pause between words to breathe as she tells the story of the previous night as coherently as possible, and Richard agreeing that they

should sort her the morning-after pill, but first they should get some rest; and, lifting up the covers for Epiphany, she climbs beneath and clings to him until – with intermittent spasms and twitching – she eventually huddles into a comatose sleep.

*   *   *

Encased in a blank and wretched nothingness as she arrives home after her much-needed rest, Epiphany feels as if she could stare at a wall or ceiling for hours and be fully entertained, such was the extent of the over-stimulation of the previous few days. Yes, that's what she would do for a while – just lie on her bed and stare at the ceiling; try to let some thoughts of her sordid adventure settle and digest (along with the morning-after pill, now sitting queasily on her tender stomach lining); to become a productive conscious thought process, something to learn from, as opposed to the hollow wretchedness now writhing away beneath her deadpan surface.

Closing the front door behind her, Epiphany pauses for a moment, listening with relief to the sweet sound of nothing – her mother must be out again. Sensing a creeping bile rise from her gut, and certain that she can't afford to lose the pill by giving into this nausea, Epiphany heads for the kitchen and, taking a bottle of mineral water from the fridge, gulps the nausea back as she heads upstairs to her room.

As her bedroom opens up before her, a jolt of surprise – choking on her water – followed by a sinking in her heart as she is greeted with a shock of dyed-black hair, a figure seated on her bed, gesturing for Epiphany to sit. Again the sickness rising with the dreaded anticipation of what is to come. Epiphany gingerly takes a seat next to her mother, who is sporting a plastic grin of mock piety and concern – *"Dear girl ...*" – running her fingers through Epiphany's hair – "*...you dear sweet pretty fool ...so much to learn.*" Epiphany pulling away from her mother, an expression of confusion on her face – "*What are you talking about?*" – swallowing again and dizzy with fatigue. "*...I pity you, I really do*" – reaching over to stroke Epiphany's face, Epiphany pushing her hand away – "*I can't handle this right now!*" – gulping harder, her mind spinning, sick with emotion – "*...please, tell me what you're talking about or leave me alone!*" Her mother's face twisting to a bitter mask – "*DON'T THINK THAT ALL MEN AREN'T BASTARDS AND PERVERTS ...BECAUSE THEY ARE!*" – rising to her feet, then resuming an expression of authoritative concern as she bends over where Epiphany is seated on the bed – "*...I know that you have betrayed me.*" Epiphany noticing her mother is holding the only pictures she has of her father; swallowing – more water – swallowing. "*...I thought he was different ...a gentle man, a kind man ...do you want to know why I divorced him?*" Swallowing – "*...Yes*" – trying to reach over to grab back the pictures; her mother quickly moving them out of her reach, then tossing them with abandon to a corner and slumping on the bed, hand on her forehead in an expression of pain and woe – "*Your father was a homosexual*" – sighing – "*...I had found a suitcase with sex toys and filthy pictures*" – her voice wavering as she speaks – "*he had been fucking ...a ...a black man*" – her face again twisting, bitter with disgust – "*...YES ...FUCKING! ...You can't call that love.*" Epiphany, struggling with her dizzying sickness, dumbfounded and shocked, not by the content of what she is hearing, but by her mother's apparent small-mindedness, feeling nothing but contempt and hatred for her mother and sadness for her father. "*...You understand, don't you dear?*" – touching her hand to Epiphany's cheek – "*...I just couldn't stand the thought of him bringing AIDS into the family.*" Epiphany's jaw dropping as the words filter slowly through the post-drug haze of her mind, her anger welling through the sedation and sickness, dizziness and nausea – *"...Get out of my room!"* Her mother hovering indignantly, an expression of hurt on her face – *"It's not easy being a single mother ...I didn't ask for this..."* Epiphany swallowing harder to muster her strength and forcing it out with a burst – *"GET OUT OF MY ROOM!"* – watching her mother's mask crack as the pantomime hurt turns to fury; determined to have the last words and hissing as she spits them out – *"You are just a child!"* – before slamming the door behind her, leaving Epiphany alone on her bed, staring blankly at the floor ...swallowing.

*   *   *

As what her mother said gradually sinks in, no great certainty comes, other than the realisation that the wretched confusion that is twisting at her gut has to be calmed somehow. As the evening draws in she decides to phone Richard, suggesting that he come round for a few drinks, as her mother will be out and they can watch some videos – the only video player in the house being in Epiphany's mother's room. Richard agrees to come round at nine, and on his arrival they head upstairs with the wine, taking off their shoes and reclining on her mother's bed to watch some of the art films Epiphany has acquired.

...They are on the second bottle of wine by the time Eraserhead has finished, its style and pacing perfectly suiting Epiphany's still warped and twisted mind. Richard had brought his bong with him, retreating to the window every ten minutes to pull one to avoid stinking out the room. Epiphany – suggesting that they watch Derek Jarman's The Garden next – ensures that Richard is seated on the bed, and that his attention is focussed as she starts the video.

At first absorbed by the flashing lights and religious imagery, Richard relaxes, slumping lower in the bed. Then – a shot of a writhing moustachioed man in bondage gear, holding a dildo – Richard remains quiet, feeling instantly self-conscious, repelled; though perhaps oddly aroused and so feeling more awkward and ashamed.

As the film progresses, Richard relaxes once more, absorbed by the images and colours dancing effervescent on his bong-addled mind. Cut to: two attractive clean-shaven men, in crisp white shirts, kissing – swell of blood to Richard's penis – mild embarrassment, so looking to Piff – afraid she can see his erection and noticing her fingering herself – relaxes. Then disappointment as the image is lost among the lights and colours. Now Richard unembarrassed about putting his hand down his pants, but disappointed to find nothing arousing in the film, just more slow-moving religious imagery; hoping again for something erotic, something forbidden… Cut to: shot of Judas hanging – tackily shot like a cheap commercial – again some weird arousal mixed with shame and Richard unsure why; finding fetishism in the image of the hanging man in leather, so forcing it out of his mind with repulsion; Epiphany laughing inwardly, aware of the effect the film is having on him. Cut to: handsome boy washing clean-shaven man's hair – Richard experiencing emotive rushing sensations of euphoric desire, before the images flash and change, cut back to clean-shaven men washing one another, naked torsos; the men kiss again as Richard wanks oblivious of Piff, who is reaching into her mother's bedside cabinet and pulling out a long white bullet of plastic and turning it on with a *BUZZZZZ* which sends lines of static across the image on the TV and – as the shot has changed to something far less interesting – instructing Richard to lie on his front and lower his pants, and Richard, closing his eyes and visualising the clean-shaven men

31

– *"I haven't done this before, be gentle."* And Epiphany smoothing her mother's Vaseline over the tip and remaining quiet as she penetrates ever so gently …Richard bites the apple.

…………The heights of painful-pleasure unimaginable, the gentle s-t-r-e-t-c-h and *BUZZZZ* as Richard is pushed, breathless, to his limits. It is the scratching of the deepest itch, scratching away all of his frustration, replacing the pain of mind with sheer sensation of body, like electricity, making each hair stand on end, energising every cell of skin, every pore opening, and as the sweet sweat pours, Richard feeling more alive than ever, one sensation sending ripples into the next, surging in waves across his whole body, until finally melting into the gush of an impossible orgasm – *"UUUHHHHHH"*…

…Epiphany withdraws her mother's vibrator and – noticing a small brown stripe down one side – gives it a gentle wipe with a tissue, and, smiling, places it back in the bedside drawer.

*   *   *

It was greeted with some relief when the blood came. She knew it would be heavy when the cramps started, wrenching at her gut mercilessly, so that all she could do was just crouch there doubled over until the pain subsided. Before the blood she thought she *could* be pregnant; unable to remember the last time her period felt this bad. At school there were always the other girls around to share in the experience – after a while it seemed that their cycles synchronized – but now Epiphany just felt alone and isolated. She had learned not to expect sympathy from her mother or her sister – *'It was Lettie who introduced me to Dan and Keith; what if I'd gotten pregnant …given birth to the mutant baby of them both …eugh!'* – and a week had passed since she last saw Richard – *'…perhaps*

he's embarrassed to contact me after last week's little episode.'
Rising to her feet to go to the toilet and feeling frail, sick and
sorry for herself as she seats herself and tugs at the cotton,
easing the blooded clump out gently. 'Seems I've left this one
in a bit long' – feeling tender in its absence, and for a moment
dangling it in front of her face, observing the depth of brown
in parts and the small clot on the end; then – as the pungency
of discharge and bad meat hits her nostrils – flushing it down
the toilet and feeling her stomach turn at the memory of the
odour still lingering on the air. Epiphany wipes herself and
inserts a new tampon, before heading to the kitchen in spite
of her sickness.

Opening the fridge with intentions towards fresh vegetables
and plenty of water; then on seeing an opened jar of prawn
mayonnaise – 'I deserve some comfort food for once' – and
tucking into the mayonnaise on a heavily buttered baguette.
For the moment, the feeling of self-pity is gone. After finishing
the prawn mayonnaise comes a gradual creeping guilt, coupled
with a sense of self-disgust. The food had tasted good, but the
increasing sense of dissatisfaction in withdrawing from the
eating experience is becoming agonising – '...Chocolate!
When was the last time I treated myself?' – so heading to the
corner shop, her mind reeling with thoughts of her favourite
sweets and cakes, as well as the cheap and nasty ones she had
enjoyed as a child – 'it's important to keep your sugar levels
up on a period' – going straight for the pick-and-mix and
sneakily eating a few before filling her bag with all sorts of
jellies and soft-centred chocolates, and putting the bag in her
basket along with a couple of king-size bars of her favourite
chocolate, then seeing the cream cakes and chocolate éclairs
– '...I am allowed to indulge this once' – and the crisps –
'...why not?' – the repressed feeling of vulnerability and self-
conscious shame still writhing away in the pit of her gut as
she makes her way to the checkout.

Arriving home again, Epiphany makes a dash for her room, fearing that her mother or sister may be there to comment on her choice of merchandise. Locking the door behind her, Epiphany empties the carrier bag onto the floor, spreading the food out in front of her and gazing at the goods, before losing herself in an éclair; sinking her teeth in slowly at first, feeling the rich chocolate-topped pastry give way to the cool cream centre, wanting that first taste – the rush of sensation as the sugar and cream and butter melt on her taste buds – to last for ever, but as the éclair is finished and she starts on the jelly sweets, a chocolate bar and the crisps, she finds a lot of the initial pleasure has gone; the refined edge of taste and sensation now blunted by the sheer quantity that is passing her lips, the enjoyment replaced by an almost mechanical desire to keep shovelling in the food, as if punishing herself for slipping up with some kind of ironic justice – gorging herself more and more until the eating process is no longer pleasurable, pushing it to the limit so the food is virtually forcing itself back out; and with the inability to eat another crumb comes again the sinking weight of self-pity.

"...Ohhh why am I such a stupid cunt?" – rising to her feet, sluggish and bloated and dragging herself to the bathroom – *'...I should've stuck with the laxatives and speed; there's no fucking way I can handle going round Dan's today'* – clenching one hand onto the ceramic of the toilet bowl, the fingers of her other making contact with the back of her throat, triggering the convulsive spasm in her gut – *"EUGGGHHHHH"* – the sweetness and salt, the bile, the brown of the chocolate and an immense feeling of dissatisfaction that the relief is not enough, the punishment is not enough, the sensation is not enough; and as the last quivering ripples of sickness shudder the length of her spine, Epiphany slumps to the floor and coils herself in her foetal pose, hoping that the darkness soon may pass.

From the pillowed comfort of his deep slumber, it seems a great amount of time must have passed since Richard and his beloved squid made their appearance on "This Morning" with Richard and Judy. They are now settled comfortably in the palatial residence on the outskirts of town that they purchased with the money from the court settlement following Richard's unfortunate incarceration. Again the feeling of love and warmth envelops Richard as he and the squid cuddle on the sofa.

Then – *BRINGGG!* – the sound of the telephone breaks their contented silence. It is a man from a Hollywood film company. Deeply moved by Richard's tale, he asks Richard if he and the squid would sell the rights to their story, explaining that the plot has all the perfect elements for a movie – *"A love that triumphs in the face of adversity and injustice."* All too aware of how infrequently man-squid relationships have been represented in the media, Richard and the squid agree that it would be a wondrous idea. The whole world must know of the purity of their love.

Again months of dreamtime pass; the anticipation building as they edge gradually closer to the day of the film's première. It will be a grand occasion. A limousine is sent to pick up Richard and the squid and escort them in luxury to this, their very special event.

Swamped and disorientated by the bright lights and glitz of the première, Richard and the squid are at first overwhelmed; then utterly dismayed as – through the barrage of flash bulbs – Richard notices that they have chosen Tom Cruise to play his role in the film – *"I hate Tom Cruise …why didn't anyone tell me?"* This dismay is shortly followed by sheer horror at the realisation that the role of his beloved golden squid has been taken by a Hollywood-friendly, conventionally attractive *human woman.* At this point Richard breaks down in tears. The director tries to console him – *"I just don't think the public is ready for a man-squid relationship yet."*

…The dream is shifting, breaking down and degenerating, swamping the squid, the warmth and the love with a barrage of repressed and fetid desires. Richard now driven by a repellent but overpowering lust as his surroundings mutate and fester and the pungency of mould and decay seeps in. Images of barren toilet walls, the stench of urine, the sense of filth and degradation, men crowding round him to take turns in abusing him, holding him down to the floor of the toilet cubicle and rubbing his face in the piss and excrement as his arse is screwed by a million filthy syphilitic cocks.

…Richard wakes, sickened, shuddering and erect; he can feel that his groin is sticky.

*   *   *

'Perhaps I should phone Richard …the fucker hasn't phoned me. I'll bet he's out somewhere getting laid by some handsome guy …some more speed would be good; I need something to lift me out of this bullshit …maybe Richard will come to Dan's with me – I'm fucked if I'm going there by myself …bad pun' – dialling Richard's number. *"Hello?"* – Richard's mother's voice, as ever warm and welcoming. *"Hello, is Richard there?"* – *"Oh hi! …No he's not here – I thought he was with you."* Pausing in thought – *"I haven't seen him for a week."* Richard's mother's voice dropping with concern – *"Oh dear …these kids, what do they get up to? …Well, when he turns up I'll let you know"* – *"Okay, thanks …bye"* – *"See you then"* – *"………………"* – and with the disengaged tone comes the

realisation that Epiphany will have to face Dan and Keith on her own – *'I'll just psych myself up with some cheap vodka first.'*

*   *   *

Waiting outside Dan and Keith's, a plastic bottle with a strong mix of vodka and orange in hand – *'It looks like they're out...'* – *"...SHIT!"* – but deciding to wait around for a bit in case they return; so laying back on the wall and swigging her drink whilst watching the sky bleed in aching pinks as the summer sun descends and dusk creeps in.

Then – barely audible at the periphery of her hearing – a familiar laugh. She sits upright, awaiting their return as the laughter and talking become clearer and Dan and Keith (and another bloke Epiphany hasn't met before) turn the corner onto their street. *"Alright girl? ...Look who come back"* – Dan's grin stretching across his face as he swaggers up the path with Keith and the other guy dragging behind him, still laughing. Epiphany just smiling demurely and standing to one side as Dan removes his keys to unlock the door.

Illuminating the humid darkness, stale with the claustrophobic smell of sweat and mouldered food, they find their seats as the fruit flies gravitate towards the light bulb. Dan fetching some beers from the fridge and passing them round before taking his seat and turning to Epiphany with a knowing look – *"So what is it then ...more billy?"* – his grin widening – *"...or somefing else?"* Epiphany smiling an awkward smile – *"Err ...just the speed."* The other guy cuts in, pointing at Dan's footwear – *"Look, the faggot fucked up your new trainers."* Dan looking at the spots on his white Reebok Classics with disgust – *"Rank! ...I hope the filfy cunt aint got AIDS or somefing."* – *"...What was that?"* – Epiphany finding his remark jarring. *"Oh nothing …just some queer cunt we caught hangin round the toilets …you should've seen his face…"* Keith still laughing – *"I reckon he fancied you."* The other bloke joining in, teasing Dan – *"Yeah, he was hot for your arse"* – *"Nah man that's rough, leave it out!"* Epiphany butts in, as a feeling of fear and sadness twists inside – *"What did he look like?"* Dan looking blankly – *"…What?"* Epiphany trying to stay calm but becoming increasingly agitated – *"How old was he? Where was it? …What did he look like?"* Dan's confusion growing – *"Fuck knows …a kid …some lanky cunt"* Her sadness turning to anger – *"WHERE?"* Dan looking at her with dismay at first, then screwing up his face in reaction to her outburst – *"…It was the bogs by the station. I don't get why it matters to you…"* But before he finishes his sentence Epiphany has scrabbled to her feet and is out the door, knocking over a beer can and the bong on her way out, and Dan shouting after her – *"YOU STUPID FUCKED-UP BITCH!"*

…Running down the hill towards the station, her mind racing through the worst possible scenarios, an emotive recollection stirring strongly at the back of her mind; the distant memory of a sensation; a hollow sinking sadness that she had not felt this strongly since it had consumed her as a child. Then passing over the railway bridge, and half afraid to look over the side for fear that she may see Richard's mutilated corpse smeared across the tracks like road-kill; and blinking the image out of her mind with desperate certainty – *'He will be okay.'* Then slowing slightly to get her breath as she approaches the men's toilets, and entering them and calling his name and kicking open the cubicle doors; noticing the pool of blood and spatters on the wall, illuminated in black under the blue of the junkie-proof light; then following the spats of blood outside for a couple of feet and losing the trail so running to a phone box and frantically dialling his home number and listening to the ring tone for endless moments, before slumping defeated on the pavement – *"Where the fuck is he?"*

…Resting her limbs for a few seconds, as her mind continues to reel, driven by the desperate need to find Richard alive, to resolve some of her loss – *'I can't let it happen again.'* So rising to her feet again, and with a fresh burst of optimism heading with determined strides towards the hill where they had tripped the previous week…

…Nearing the top of the hill she can just make out a figure seated on the bench, with his head bowed as if deep in thought; her hope gradually melting into relief as she begins to make out Richard's familiar form. Taking a seat next to him she places her hand on his. He remains indifferent, staring blankly at the ground. *"Richard?"* – Epiphany speaking calmly so he doesn't feel pressurised into saying anything – *"…I know what happened."* Richard lifts his face to her so it is illuminated beneath the lamplight. Epiphany is at first startled; his cheekbones seem raised and his complexion pale; his lips are full and swollen with blood, and his eyes are softly blossoming in shades of purple that darken at the bridge of the nose. For the first few seconds his whole appearance seems almost beautifully feminine, like a caricature of Marilyn Monroe, but her perception of the face as something beautiful is only fleeting, as she observes that the front of Richard's clothes are black with crusted blood – *"are you okay? …Should we go to the hospital?"* Richard slowly breaking out of his blank introversion – *"I don't want to go to hospital…"* – as he slowly becomes animated, he lifts back his sleeve to show Epiphany the cuts on his arm – *"…they'll ask questions"* – grinning back at her with a crazed look in his eye, his grin reopening the split on his lip and staining his teeth with fresh blood – *"…I'll be okay"* – before resuming his silent staring at the ground.

"…It took me ages to find you; you should've called or something" – Epiphany looking down at the lights coming on in the town below, awaiting a response, but hearing nothing but the hum of distant cars – *"…well say something Richard, I've been fucking worried – I thought you might have done something stupid like…"* – *"KILLED MYSELF?!"* – spitting the words at her with a spray of saliva and blood – *"…I probably should've!"* Richard's words grating deeply on Epiphany as her initial sadness quickly turns to contempt and anger at his sentiment – *"DON'T BE SO FUCKING SELF-PITYING …HOW DO YOU THINK THAT MAKES ME FEEL?"* Richard blanking her words and rolling his eyes as he lashes out at the air and tears his fingers into the soil, wishing that he could have the strength to end it all but feeling weak inside his flesh, so arching his back and gazing up in hatred at the infinite sky, angry at his insignificance, then down at the town dwarfed below with its hundreds of windows of light, and wondering if there can be anyone out there who could begin to understand him – *"…THIS TOWN IS SUCH A FUCKING SHITHOLE!"* – the sound of his voice echoing on the distant streets – *"…some days I just feel like doing something really fucked up, to shake up this"* – scratching at his face and gesturing madly to the sky – *"…I mean, we're supposed to be almost adults and what does this mean? … Pretend that were all grown up now… I'm just as unsure …no, more unsure about the world and what or who I am than I have ever been"* – his voice cracking – *"I don't know shit … I'm frightened. I mean what the fuck am I supposed to be? I feel guilty for being me …in school the word gay is the biggest insult in use; the other kids spit on me and call me a queer or a fag and I've always insisted I wasn't and insulted them back …but now I feel like giving in … I am a fag"* – shouting at the top of his voice – *"I AM A FAG! … I like to get my arse fucked"* – his swollen face illuminated beneath the lamplight – *"…IT'S ALL FUCKING SHIT!"* Epiphany trying to calm

40

him but finding him too engrossed in his rage. *"…It's like these terms people use like 'red-blooded man', y'know: 'he likes his women he's a red-blooded man' …SO WHAT THE FUCK AM I THEN? A FUCKING LIZARD?!"* – slamming his palm into his nose to reiterate his point with a fresh flow of blood, then wincing in pain and spitting in disgust and laughing and crying, the blood bubbling from his nose. Epiphany again angered by his pathetic display of self-abuse – *"DO YOU THINK YOU'RE THE ONLY PERSON IN THE WORLD WHO HAS PROBLEMS AND THE THOUGHTS YOU HAVE!?"* Richard calming, shocked by her reaction – *"I've only ever been myself and I don't even know how to be me properly …WHY AM I NOT JUST LIKE EVERYONE ELSE?"* – *"RICHARD! …We're all fucking different …it's what makes us unique …you are so much stronger for being you …in spite of those arseholes!"* A slight smile breaks on Richard's lips, only to be crushed again by the weight of his thoughts – *"But I don't know how to do the gay thing …I mean I'm not sure I enjoy it …I get off on the sensation, but I'm always left with this emptiness …The men who I wank off …who I've let shag me, are often so repulsive to me"* – taking a deep breath – *"…I do want the sex and I put myself into the situation to get it …but I feel degraded… it's not because I find them attractive and want to have sex with them, it's because I've gotten used to feeling like I'm worthless …it's easier to feel repulsed by yourself than to feel respect for yourself…"* – cringing – "*the men who I actually find attractive in this town are often the same types who would hate me for who I am …It's like when those guys came into the toilet earlier – I saw one at first, and to start with I thought I was going to meet someone who wasn't my dad's age …then he started laying into me… and then his mates came… and I…"* – crying through his nose – *"…I just remember slumping down on the floor and they were kicking me and…"* – looking upwards with agonizing despair – *"…and as they laid into me I imagined they were fucking me… and for those moments it felt okay, and all the pain was gone…"*

…Covering his face in the folds of his arms and weeping and weeping, aware that his wallowing can only enforce the cloying sense of utter futility, but unable to express himself in any other way. After a few moments Epiphany opens her mouth to speak – *"Look at me, Richard"* – lifting his face to hers – *"…we are way too fucking big for this town …it doesn't have to be like this …we've got a great future; this town is nothing …it's just a speck on our lives"* – smiling at him – *"…when you're not all beaten up you're very handsome …and soon when school is over you can move to Brighton or London or someplace where you can be who the fuck you want …the boys will be all over you."*

…And Epiphany – sensing Richard warm to her words as they slowly melt his shell of introversion – now feeling some resolve, the completeness that she had not felt since her childhood. So wrapping her arms around him, and he embracing her back, and as they open themselves to one another for the first time in Richard's awareness, a simple realization filters gently to the surface of his conscious mind, from which it seems to resonate throughout – *'I am not alone …I am alive …I am alive.'*

DEATH RATTLE

The present, I hold only in contempt
For it is now and now and always now
Whereas the past embroiders on itself
With recollection's corners worn by time

The future holds its openness unwrit
It is a breath that has yet to be breathed
Or that of death; to suffocate diseased
When what was planned reveals the opposite

Now's sad stone certainty, I scrutinise
Whereas the times of joy just seem to fleet
Sit back on life, relax and close your eyes
Until nostalgia brings life back, complete

＊   ＊   ＊

INTRODUCTION

Every time I get a sore throat I get frightened, frightened that
the sore throat will lead to a cough, that the cough will lead to
a cold, that the cold will lead to an illness, and before I know
it, I'm back in hospital with my very life in jeopardy and the
sense that it was all so brief, that I could have done so much
more. I don't want to live with this morbid sense of impending doom, that at any time my body's defences could begin to
deteriorate again and it would be left to my parents to pick up
the pieces. They don't want to have me to worry about. They
have a beautiful new granddaughter (my niece); they can't
take my problems on board when she's running around and
growing and getting stronger. In my niece, my sister has created something so simple yet so constructive; she has utilised

the in-built drive within all creatures (sex) for its true means, to create more life. I got it all wrong: sex for me became an act of self-destruction. This was never a lifestyle choice; I just never had an excuse to feel strong and happy with myself. In the light of my recent illness I feel that now I do. Maybe I can't feel truly happy for myself and the path my life has taken, but I feel for the good of myself and those around me that I *must* start to approach life with a more optimistic outlook, or else condemn myself to death. I cannot overestimate the potential of my self-destruction; I have come too close. This piece of writing serves as a rationalising and exorcising of that self-destructive spirit. I hope it can stand on its own as something constructive beyond my own indulgence.

Oliver Speer, June 2001.

*   *   *

PART ONE: DEAD END, 1998

Standing on the edge of nowhere, looking on to somewhere, is where I want to be. Poised, ready to take on board any possibility, any conceivable route, this is the place where I thrive. Today, however, I feel I have met a dead end. A dead end of inevitability, endless predictable drudgery. All the backrooms, bars and toilets call me back, mocking me with old routines of cock and suck and drug and fuck. What once started as a quest for experience, an exercising of individual freedom, has turned out to be a trap. The mind has its confines and limits – we can only reach so far, dig so deep, until we reach a mud so thick and cloying that we find ourselves stuck, and start sinking.

I have been sinking for many years now, sucked in by my own futile quest to find something beyond, something divine; driven by my own hunger and lust, a slave to my sex drive. The insecure striving for contact, to touch, to feel a part of someone else, something else, to absorb a part of everyone. And as soon as you realise no one holds the answer, no one can save you, or lift you up, or guide you, you get bitter and cynical and feel powerless, and let more people fuck you up, fuck you over, fuck you, just to rub salt into the wound, just to verify your powerlessness. Not wanting to accept responsibility, it helps you to feel weak from time to time; it's easier – abandon all control for fate and experience.

One time you ask a rough-looking skinhead to tie you up, just to see what it's like. Hog-tied, wrist to ankles, you tell him the safe word is "cunt" (easily distinguishable) – when you say "cunt", whatever happens, he must stop. He inserts a finger into your anus; his hands are coarse and dry, you wince. He inserts another two fingers. *"Careful!" – "Try to relax."* Soon all his fingers are inside you; he's playing rough and your eyes start watering. He begins to make his hand into a fist. This is territory you don't want to go near. *"CUNT!...FUCKING CUNT!"* – you gasp. He just smiles and delves deeper. *"CUNT! CUNT! Pleeease! CUNT"* – tears running down your cheeks. Unable to move – restricted by the bands bonding your wrists to your ankles. It feels like your hip is going to dislocate; agonising discomfort – *"CUUUNT!!!"* He stops and slowly withdraws and unties you. Shaking and feeling physically sick, you swallow and force out a sentence – *"I said 'cunt', I kept saying 'cunt', we agreed that was the word" – "You wanted me to go just that little bit further"* – he says – *"come next week you'll be thinking back to this night and having a good old wank."*

…Perhaps, it's too soon to tell. Shaken and wretched, I look round the room for my clothes, and gather them, unable to look my aggressor in the eye. A sock is lying in a pool of vomit. *'Fucking all time low'* – I think desperately, breaking for a moment through the psychotic haze of three-day speed. I stand up, causing the blood to rush from my head – momentary blackout. The sensation surges over me, and with it come the memories of that evening. The sick is on the floor because the skinhead had wanted to vomit on my penis whilst sucking me off. Seeing as my self-destructive streak had thrown me into kamikaze experience mode, I agreed to let him, but found I had to ask him to stop after only a few seconds because the half-digested chunks tangled in my pubes made me feel ill, and my vomiting would not be wise, seeing as I hadn't eaten since Thursday. The skinhead obligingly urinated on me to wash the vomit off. I had been aware of piss fetishes, but not so much vomit. Although I wasn't actively interested, I always said I'd try anything once – something to tell your grandchildren when you're in the nursing home.

*   *   *

PART TWO: 2000

I started that last piece of writing two years ago with the intention of creating a short story. After those few paragraphs I had to stop as it became too painful. I have, since the aforementioned incident (though not because of it), contracted HIV, and now find myself emaciated and languishing in a hospital bed with tuberculosis death rattle rasping from my lungs. At one moment my body is shuddering in indescribable cold, and the next pouring out sweat like a tap, whereupon the sheets have to be changed (this happens numerous times throughout the night).

The depths of this illness are a blur. I don't remember much, except for the religious hallucinations; a bearded Jesus face will appear in the random textures of a wall, for instance, or a figure of the Virgin illuminated behind closed eyelids. For fear of becoming a self-righteous born-again Christian upon my recovery, I have to tell myself these hallucinations are merely archetypal images which every mind carries, and which are only revealed at times when the mind phases out and weakens; Christianity having utilised these archetypes for its own ends. I am on a lot of blood and have also hallucinated tigers – giant fluid tigers morphing from the blood bag suspended by my bed and leaping over me from left to right. This experience became so intense that I had to call for the nurse. I rang the small buzzer to the right of my bed and the nurse entered. *"I'm aware of hallucinations – I've experienced them before, but there are these giant blood tigers leaping over my bed and I'm wondering if I should do anything about it…"* The rather camp male nurse paused to think – *"…Is this upsetting you?"* In these sterile surroundings the hallucinations are actually a refreshing change, and, due to my altered state, the presence of the nurse was becoming stranger than they were – *"It's a bit intense but I think I can cope"* – I reply. *"Well, I probably shouldn't give you any more drugs. If it continues, give me a bell and we'll see if we can get a doctor to have a look at you."* The tigers continued throughout the night but I decided not to bother the nurse, and in time I had fallen asleep.

*   *   *

In the midst of this disease I am somehow coping. When ill the human mind locks into another drive of consciousness and existence, and a lot of the self shuts down so that the body and mind can put all of their energies into the healing process. When I was first taken ill with this sickness, we thought it was only the side effects of the anti-retroviral medication I had been advised to start taking. It started with flu-like symptoms and problems with the circulation in my

47

legs. For a time I could walk only with a stick, and later my walking became so pained that I had to be taken to bed at my mother's house.

My body's defences, however, had started deteriorating *before* I was made to take the anti-retrovirals. Although I was aware on some level that I was becoming weak, I must have been in denial, as I was still trying to keep up with my friends' drinking and partying. Often at night, after going out to a club and consuming copious amounts of booze and ecstasy, I would find myself waking up in the warmth of my own urine. This was particularly embarrassing if I was sharing my bed with a friend, as was often the case. I clearly remember several occasions where I found myself inadvertently urinating on good friends of mine. The friends would always be polite, saying nothing of the dampness the next day. Most of the time a lot of the moisture had dried out by then anyway, as I would wake up just as I realised I was pissing, and would cuddle close to my friend in an attempt to evaporate most of the fluid with our body heat before they woke up.

For the two bedridden weeks at my mother's house (just before I was checked into hospital) I observed the breaking down of the facets of my ego. Constantly running a fever and hallucinating, I imagined at one time six distinct characters in the bed with me, all facets of my own personality. One was that of my sister in her youth, argumentative and bossy. Others were more literal alter egos that I had at one time consciously created. These included Geoffrey, anal yet self-destructive, insular and numb; the debauched priest or preacher; and the porn ego I created when earning some money to get through the first year of college. (His name, "Richard Eastwood", was an amalgam of the names of the first friends I told about the porn film.) I rarely feel consistent in my ego or persona, but in those first two weeks of hallucinatory sickness it seemed that all of the facets of myself were simultaneously rising to the surface, fighting it out amongst themselves in my deluded half-sleep tangle of dream and reality. It was as if I was sweating these facets of my personality out, to prepare myself for the ego-less state so important to the healing process.

My sister had become pregnant shortly after my diagnosis. She had decided to keep the baby, partly for my mother's sake, to soften the blow when she heard my bad news. This was a gesture made with good intent, though I can't help feeling that the baby is to be my replacement.

My mother had given me a lift up to London to have my check up. Afterwards we had hoped to be among the first to see my newborn niece. The doctors were amazed that I had not been checked into hospital long ago. We told them that we thought I was simply adjusting to the anti-retrovirals. They said there was no way I should be visiting a newborn baby in my condition, and promptly had me admitted as an in-patient. My mother feels torn between wanting to spend time with me and wanting to support my sister. Both her children checked into hospital on the same day, one for matters of birth and the other, death.

I had been making attempts at recording the experience – before being checked into hospital I was sketching my emaciated form, and since then have made records of my deterioration. I have also stolen a catheter and several syringes as souvenirs. I imagine I might incorporate them into an art piece if I recover; however, in my sickened, ego-less state the concept of art seems absurd, as does life in general.

This loss of self and ego is a state aspired to by many religions. The wretchedness of conscious life is at times so unbearable we do all we can do to shut off the mechanism: chanting, meditation, drugs. Sleep is rarely salvation. My dreams offer me a mirror. When life is bad I often sleep well, only to wake to the dawning realization of the shit I'm in. Equally, when life is good with nothing to worry about, my dreams find reasons to torment me; I may wake in a cold sweat from a nightmare that the cheese in the fridge might be past its sell-by date and I haven't eaten it yet. And I come to, and think to myself, why am I doing this? What have I got to worry about?

I believe that human life is tormented from the outset and that we, as human beings, will go out of our way to find problems, something to contend with, to validate our torment and misery and make our existence more tangible. Do you think those millions who wept in mourning at the death of Princess Diana were really crying for a person they had never met? I believe we use these occasions as an excuse to vent our own misery and frustration; in reality we are weeping for ourselves.

In my case, at least, I find that when I have a real problem I am far more focussed, and when I don't I find myself desperately struggling to find meaning in my existence. Enveloped in this sickness, I find all my struggles and conflicts are gone. I am in that oblivious state of limbo so yearned for; I am Zen, I merely exist, my body aches but my mind is free of pain. I feel my life, so brief and insignificant, seep through my pores, and all to me is meaningless. But somehow I don't mind.

*   *   *

The HIV has become me – it now seems it was inevitable, like destiny. This disease is perpetuated by sexual acts, though the illness has drained me of any sex drive. On one level this is quite liberating, as I can't remember the last time I went five minutes without thinking about sex. In this state sex seems the most absurd concept of them all. I wonder what a family tree of all the people who contracted HIV would look like, who fucked who and how it got to me.

HIV remains synonymous with the gay scene. It is relatively recently that homosexuality was made legal. As it existed for many years as something underground and secret, sexual encounters were often brief and anonymous, a stigma the gay scene has found hard to shake off.

The scene is full of different and unusual sexual practices. This is not because gay men are intrinsically more perverse than your average heterosexual man, but because homosexuality itself has for many years been deemed a perversion and something to be hidden away and swept under the carpet. The gay man, on confronting his sexuality and revealing his true self, will have confronted the biggest hurdle of his life. When one comes to terms with himself on this level, all minor perversions, fetishes and vices that the average heterosexual would repress will also rise to the surface. For this reason, what is underground within straight culture is mainstream within gay culture – pretty much anything goes.

As male sexuality is very different from female sexuality, a man and a woman will often have to go through a number of social courtship rituals before they have sex. But when a man is attracted to another man, a lot of the rituals associated with heterosexual bonding and courtship can be short-circuited. Thus places exist (and have done since the beginning of time) where men can meet solely for sex. On the surface this can seem a great idea – free sex on tap. But the gay teenager who – unaware how else to meet others like himself – naively wanders into such an environment looking for his first loving relationship, is likely to find instead (as happens all too often on the scene) that once someone's fucked you they lose interest. This often enforces the sense of isolation that many young gay men feel.

*   *   *

I have had a considerably high sex drive for as long as I can remember. Even as a child I was tormented by fetishistic visions and impulses that I couldn't begin to understand. From the age of being sexually active I was aware of the dangers of sex, so made sure that if I was looking for it I always carried a condom.

Things can get out of hand, though. Too many drugs – fat lines of coke – and the guy is gorgeous; I have so much respect for him – he's an author, and older and stronger than me, and he tells me I'm beautiful and he'll take care of me and he loves me. Of course I don't believe a word of it, but I let myself get caught up in the romance of the evening; there is so much ahead. So he takes me to a club; he's on the guest list and all the drinks are free. We drop a few pills, more charlie, poppers. I end up back at his flat, a grand luxurious flat with a pristine king-sized bed as the centrepiece. This guy, before becoming a writer, first established himself in the world of gay porn. Though I can't remember the names of any of his films, his image was prolific, and on more than one occasion provided me with momentary relief from my teenage frustrations. And there I was, about to *actually* have sex with him.

Although my recollection of the night is foggy to say the least, I *do* remember insisting that he use a condom, and getting a strong impression that he felt put out by this request. He was not aware that I knew that he was HIV positive. When I was fifteen I had accidentally recorded a late-night TV interview with him, which I found myself rewinding repeatedly, wearing out the tape and using up a lot of tissues with it.

He says something about lubricating the inside of the condom because it feels nice. It hurts to start with, but as the drugs and poppers have loosened me up I'm soon lost in the most incredible sensations, and so am pained to tell him to stop when I sense something is wrong and soon realise that the condom is no longer there. He seems annoyed that I made him stop. Not wanting to upset him, I tell him to try again with a fresh condom. When, after a time, I find that condom to be missing as well, I become quite distressed. I tell him that I know he is positive. I remember him becoming defensive, and the atmosphere turning unpleasant and conversation awkward. The next morning he was quick to chuck me out.

Later, when I go to the toilet, the condoms come out, entwined in my faeces; the rubberised clump won't flush, so I have to remove it by hand. Desperately in need of advice and support I try to contact him, but only get an answering machine. I leave a message but don't hear anything back. I book myself an appointment at the clinic.

HIV is known to be present when the relevant antibodies kick in. This usually takes about three months. They test me to see if I have HIV already; a week later the results arrive – negative. Three months later I'm sitting in the clinic again, waiting for results. The woman who enters is smiling – maybe a bit nervously, but a smile nonetheless. It can't be bad news. She speaks casually, retaining her fixed grin – *"Well the test came back and it's positive, you are entitled to counselling, should you fall ill you can refuse any medication if you wish, you will be asked to return monthly for a check up, only you don't come in here you go to the clinic in the basement. Any questions?"*

My friend Corrina is with me. She starts crying. I'm quite taken aback. No questions spring to mind. We go to the pub.

PART THREE: HELL ON SEA

I come from the coastal town of Hastings; the memory of the grey salt sea lingers strong in my nostrils. The seafront façades, once the height of Edwardian glamour, are now gutted crumbling shells. Down on the promenade the drunks sway and spurt obscenities, lovingly cradling their bottles of White Lightning and cans of Special Brew.

Once, when I was young, I found out that the toilets dotting the seafront were a cruising ground for queers. At the time my burgeoning sexuality, which I had not yet fully confronted, was becoming a great burden to me (the minds of most fifteen year-olds being somewhat tormented anyway). These sordid underground encounters, with old perverted pederasts and men who could not tell their families of their true nature, seemed in fitting with the guilt and shame I had long felt.

Since then all for me is out in the open and well vented. Since then the council have dotted the seafront with cameras, and so many police patrol the town that a constant violation of one's privacy is taken for granted. At one time the promenade was rife with sexual encounters, smack addicts; a rainbow of debauchery (addicts and helpless cases are moved to the town for cheap B&B and the dole). Extra policing never solves the problem, it just moves it somewhere else, forces it further underground. We once enjoyed happy hour down at Cherry's (a local bar), until someone got stabbed and the police (believing they'd got the culprit and that he was armed) raided a flat and shot dead an innocent (and naked) man. After that Cherry's was closed down. I kind of miss the fist fights and glasses flying around; cheap beer and snakebite consumed by the gallon, sustained with mountains of amphetamine.

"HELL ON SEA" is what the papers called Hastings after the deputy head of a local school beat his adopted daughter to death with a tent peg. Murder and rape are commonplace. The locals often talk of a curse put on the town by the occultist Alistair Crowley, the legacy of this curse being that it is difficult, if not impossible, for the town's inhabitants to ever leave. Following his death his house on the hill was burned down. Where it stood is now waste ground.

From my hospital bed I think fondly of Hastings, and wonder what keeps drawing me back to a town so choked with the stench of hopelessness, unemployment, suicide and despair – a town that is so much a part of me.

* * *

Before my illness I was arrested on the way to a squat party in London. We were just going to set up the rig when our car was pulled over. The police had me on some hash (just an eighth in my tobacco pouch), while a friend of mine was found with ketamine and a small amount of opium. We had been cooking up the K beforehand and I had written poems and slogans on the inside of the wraps, such as – *"Phone your mother you filthy K-head"*. These were to be read when the wrap was finished, the users having dug themselves a sizeable hole. On reading these slogans one officer said to another – *"What's this about then?"* To which the other knowingly replied – *"Trademarks"* – revealing the average policeman's inept sense of humour.

I was strip searched; DNA samples were taken; fingerprints and mug shots. The police seemed quite taken aback about my HIV. *"So how did you get that then?"* – said one officer in an arrogant and condescending tone. *"Someone took advantage of me"* – was my curt reply. At this the officer apologised and remained silent.

On searching my pockets I was aware I had nothing to declare. Unlike the time two years earlier, when I was arrested on acid in Hastings for stealing wood for a beach party bonfire. On this occasion, whilst in the police van, I transferred a wrap of speed from my wallet to my shoe, all the time making conversation with five police officers, a three-day cocktail of drugs coursing through my mind and body.

In the cell I learned how to meditate. Before incarceration they handed me a list of the formalities I could expect should I be tried in court (their intention being to make me stew in my own guilt). They also told me to leave my shoes (with the speed) outside my cell. I was tripping, and realised that no amount of worrying would help the situation or my future mental health, so, ignoring the list, I spent the next four hours humming an improvised mantra to accompany the infinite geometric patterns emerging from within.

"So how did you find that then?" – an officer asked aggressively, before escorting me to be interviewed. *"Really good!"* – was my reply – *"I rarely get an opportunity to meditate."* In the interview room my solicitor was more condescending than the police – *"Just admit to stealing the wood and we can go home."* His voice had the tired lilt of a man who had better things to do than waste his time on idiots like me. I told him that I wouldn't have taken the wood had I known it was someone's property (it had turned out to be the shutters of the building it was leaning against). *"Don't waste our time"* – was my solicitor's exasperated reaction. I was encouraged to lie – saying that I knowingly stole the shutters – so that the case wouldn't go to court. I was then awarded with a caution, and, after a few photographs were taken, the guard told me I could put my shoes back on. I remember my relief as my toes touched the wrap of speed.

I finally made it to the beach party at seven or eight a.m. A couple of friends were gathered, still tripping by the fire's last burning embers. I was offered a spliff. It tasted great – *'So this is how freedom feels.'*

*   *   *

When, as a child, I first learned to write, I wrote from right to left in mirror image. I only got as far as writing my name in this manner, as I was quickly weaned off it. This upset me because, if it was my true nature, surely it should have been encouraged. For years I imagined that perhaps, as a baby, I had been replaced by the mirror child. This would explain why I felt so different to everyone else.

At around the age of three, I would say to my mother that I wanted to die (though today I have no concept of a three year-old's knowledge of death). I had awful nightmares in which I scratched my face with my nails, sobbing and tormented. My mother would pick me up like a bundle, holding me warm and close; she'd comfort me, telling me how good Christmas would be when it comes. I'd drift back to sleep, clinging to those warm thoughts of optimism: Christmas does come round again, life does get better. It will all turn out all right.

In primary school I had few friends and did anything I could to get out of going. On more than one occasion I remember drinking shampoo to make me sick so I didn't have to attend. My bowels had long been a problem. My lower intestine was distended and would not grow at the same rate as the rest of my body. This caused me great pain and frequent problems. One such problem, anal thrush at about the age of eight, involved treatment which entailed filling a large plastic syringe with foam and injecting the foam into my anus. When the thrush had cleared I found pleasure in using the plastic syringe to inject warm water into my bowels. At that age I had no knowledge of enemas or the hidden pleasures of the rectum. Bowel cleansing became a habit for a couple of weeks. The only problem being that the warm brown water would gush down my leg when least expected. Because of this my mother took me back to the doctor. The doctor said it was probably the side effects of the medication and should wear off after a time. For those weeks I was made to wear a sanitary towel. I also got the time off school.

Being young I knew very little of homosexuality. I do remember that my father, who had spent some time in the marines, often associated homosexuality with paedophilia, talking of how, when on leave, he and his mates would beat up a queer and nick his money. (I have since cleared the air with him and we now get on very well.) These comments, which greatly affected me, continued on a regular basis up until several years ago, when my father must have realised that I was beyond redemption. From a young age I was acutely aware that I was different. I remember praying that I wouldn't turn into one of those people that I thought my father hated.

At school I found myself experiencing strong emotions towards other boys. This, I told myself, was because I wanted to be like them. I got erections at all sorts of bizarre things I didn't understand – masculine associated things: vehicles, sports, items of clothing. This disturbed me greatly, and in my confusion I often cried myself to sleep.

Somewhere towards the end of my thirteenth year I came across a clothes catalogue belonging to my sister. All the other boys at school talked of wanking, but I had never tried. I turned to the women's underwear section and stared intently at the models posing in skimpy lingerie, whilst mauling my genitals for stimulation. I was not getting a hard-on. Without consciously regarding what I was doing I turned to the men's section. That was when everything started happening. The sensations I was feeling were unlike anything I had experienced – a scratching of an impossible itch. In time the welling up of all my desire and frustration reached an extreme melting tension, only to explode and shoot across the room to the opposite wall.

The next sensation to pass over me was a combination of heart-sinking guilt and shame. It was now definite – I was a queer, a faggot, a homo, a poof. In my paranoid teenage mind I was everything my father, and everyone in every school, in every town, hated and wanted dead.

After that first ejaculation I had remembered one incident at the age of around ten, which I had blocked from my mind, as I couldn't make sense of it at the time. In the excitement of play I had kissed my best friend on the cheek. In an instant the fun had turned aggressive – my friend started calling me a queer and saying I was gay (terminology I didn't then associate with myself). He then got some other "friends" to hold me down and hold my legs open while he kicked me squarely and repeatedly in the balls.

Naturally I couldn't tell my school friends of my epiphany. In the school yard the word "gay" is commonly used to describe anything crap, unworthy or insufficient. I couldn't live with this tag, so I went out of my way to have relationships with girls to prove to my friends, and to myself, that I was straight.

One day, on my way back from school, I stopped by a public toilet, as I needed a shit. I entered the graffiti-covered cubicle, dropped my pants and sat down. I had seen stuff written on toilet walls before, but being naive and paranoid I thought it was probably written by the police, or men who would beat up whoever they caught responding to the messages. I reached for the toilet roll and jumped, startled. Above the toilet roll dispenser was a hole in the chipboard wall, through which was peering an eye. My heart jumped into my throat, pounding tenfold. I quickly wiped my arse, then bunked myself up onto the toilet so I could see over into the neighbouring cubicle.

What I saw was a fat middle-aged man in tweed, with a flat cap, hurriedly adjusting his fly. I didn't know for how long he'd been watching me, but from his flushed expression I knew he'd been masturbating. Experiencing a rush of nausea through my whole body, I darted out of the toilet and ran all the way home.

From the age of fourteen I masturbated compulsively, often three or four times a day, just to get the lustful thoughts out of my head, to calm the demon. At that age I also went for long walks of an evening along the seafront.

My first sexual experience was at about this age. I was reading the writing on a toilet cubicle along the Marina when I heard a man enter to urinate. He had been standing by the urinals for some time when I heard his feet move towards my cubicle. He made two pronounced snorting noises. I had not seen what he looked like, but through curiosity I emulated his noises, to which he coughed. This I also repeated. I had seen it written on the wall that this kind of communication is common practice, though I was quite taken aback when the door of my cubicle opened.

The man who stood before me was plain-looking, probably in his mid-thirties, with a slim, almost skinny build. He whispered in a rasping voice – *"I know a place where we can go."* My heart was beating fast and the feeling of nausea was there, but at the same time I felt somewhat exhilarated. *"Okay"* – I said. He left the cubicle looking behind at me and I nervously followed.

We walked for quite some time. He asked my name and if I had a boyfriend. I told him I had a girlfriend. *"I meet lots like you"* – he said. We finally reached a beach hut further up the beach. He said it belonged to a friend. He unlocked the door of the whitewashed shack. It had no lights, the floor was damp and there was no furniture, so we had to stand. He kissed me; his flesh and saliva felt cold and reptilian. He slowly unzipped my fly and reached inside. I was erect; his hand felt clammy.

When, after some fumbling, I ejaculated, the horror of what I was doing came over me. I quickly made my excuses and left. I retched at the thought of what I had done and couldn't spit enough to get his taste out of my mouth.

I would return to the seafront sporadically as the months passed. I was very depressed, and the bad sex somehow made me feel better about my depression – it gave it a reason and validated it. At that time I toyed with lame suicide attempts; I also cut myself.

On one rare occasion I actually met an attractive boy of about my age. He told me he was straight and he just wanted someone to suck him off. All I wanted was to kiss him and hold him and lie with him. He told me I couldn't kiss him; he just wanted his cock sucked. It was shaped like a banana.

After leaving school and coming-out (aged seventeen) to my friends and mother, I had some brief relationships. These often consisted of straight boys who wanted to experiment but who, when it came down to it, were really straight, and so fucked with my emotions. Or boys who were probably really gay but had girlfriends, so our encounters were sworn to secrecy lest anyone find out. These all seemed in some way tainted with self-destruction and self-loathing, often not on my part. One boy, who I realise in retrospect I was in love with, claimed to be very suicidal. I didn't believe him as he was something of a faker; he went through religions like shirts. I called his bluff and said – *"If you're going to do it, do it properly. Try two techniques at once – take some pills and hang yourself."* We split up after a time. He was found a month later in his hometown, hung by the neck. He had also taken an overdose.

*   *   *

PART FOUR: FADE OUT

These memories come back to me in hospital; I am in quarantine so there's not much else to think about. I have gotten very good at shutting off my mind and staring at the wall for hours, as I can't seem to tune in the TV. It would only be mindless trivia anyway. I feel I must soak up this experience. I have started to decline my three-hourly fix of codeine.

Many medications have been tried and failed, including "Septrin", a drug that, when drip-fed, felt as its name sounds – a septic acid burning through my veins, causing the needle entry points to get infected, leaving me with sores up my arms. At first they thought I had pneumonia, then PCP (which I thought was a drug), then they decided I had tuberculosis. It was a relief when they stopped the Septrin, but I did not anticipate what was to replace it.

The tuberculosis and anti-retroviral medication I have been prescribed consists of over twenty pills, ranging from small ones to what looks like a horse tranquilliser. I have to take these pills before breakfast. I am often sick, and as a result am made to take them again. My throat is raw with bile and the dry scrape of numerous tablets. On top of this, most of the veins in my arms have collapsed due to the constant drip-feeds and injections. This has caused my gaunt limbs to take on a bluish hue, dotted with purple-yellow bruises. On one occasion the nurse came to give me an injection, I felt the needle enter the vein then exit into the wasted muscle on the other side. Despite my whimpers of protest the nurse proceeded to empty the syringe into my flesh. My arm ached in agony, a swollen purple balloon that felt like it might fall off.

The doctor has ordered me another chest x-ray – about the fifth in as many weeks. I am wheeled there as I am wheeled everywhere. The only exercise I get is the walk to the toilet, and due to this I have now fully lost the use of my legs. On the way to x-ray, waiting for the elevator, a young girl of about five or six stares at me in my wheelchair, oxygen cylinder and mask attached. I can sense she is frightened – I must look pretty scary. My eyes and cheekbones are sunken and my frame has the gauntness of death. I stare back at her and hold my gaze, watching her shiver in terror as if she is about to cry. Her parents pull her away.

Outside x-ray I keep nodding off. With no space to rest in my wheelchair, my head rolls back and I awaken with a start.

The results show my heart has gotten bigger. I make some joke, such as – *"Does that mean I'm a more loving person?"* The doctors mumble a wry chuckle in response. *"It seems your heart has got infected. The sack that surrounds it has inflated with fluid to fight off the infection."* I was not surprised – my heartbeats had been pained and my breathing shallow. I was told the fluid had to be drained as soon as possible.

The next day I had an appointment to see the surgeon. I had to have the last slot in the day to prevent my TB from being passed to any other patients. I was supposed to be starved of food and water for twelve long hours beforehand, but as the appointment was put back it was more like twenty. I don't mind the lack of food, as I haven't been eating anyway, but the lack of fluids is unbearable, as I've been on oxygen for days, which tends to dry your mouth out.

I am wheeled into a room and surrounded by surgeons and medical students. I am told my condition is rare, and that the procedure I require involves draining off the fluid constricting my heart through a tube fed underneath my ribcage. This, I am told, is a risky procedure, and so I must sign legal forms accepting the possibility of death. One of the students asks how old I am. *"Twenty-two"* – I reply. *"You're so young, it's such a shame"* – she says, enforcing the sense of impending doom.

I am placed on a foam wedge and given an injection of local anaesthetic. My heart is visible on the monitor above my head. I am disinfected. The surgeon explains that he will make a small incision through which a wire will be fed. This wire will be visible on the monitor as it cuts its way to my heart. When it hooks in place the tube can be fed in, ready to drain the fluid. *"If my heart stops beating and you have to prize open my ribcage, will I still be conscious?"* – I enquire, only half-jokingly. *"It's not funny – you mustn't speak like that"* – snaps the surgeon.

I am awake for the whole process, and can see it all taking place. In spite of the local anaesthetic I can feel the incision and every move the wire makes. I watch in the monitor as the end of the wire hooks in place between the sack containing the fluid and my heart. The surgeon attaches a large syringe and starts syringing out the fluid – it is green-yellow in colour, like pungent urine. Each syringe is put aside to be sent to a laboratory. After a few I ask if it's nearly finished. *"We've only just started"* – the surgeon says.

Syringe after syringe after syringe is set aside. I can literally feel the pressure being released from around my heart. When the procedure is finished I ask the surgeon how much fluid there was. *"About two litres"* – he replies – *"that's the same as two cartons of orange juice."* I have to sleep for two nights with the tube attached and a bag draining any remaining fluid. Every time my heart beats I can feel the wire scratching against it.

*   *   *

I often carry with me the burden that the whole path I took from my teenage years (away from my mother, to whom I felt very close) was some search for conflict; a stirring-up of my boring, middle class, middle of the road life; to give myself a cause, something to feel passionate about, something that matters. From this point I threw myself into wretched experiences – a mental self-mutilation. Drugs, sex, dressing like a freak, getting beaten up and going out even weirder the next night to show I didn't care and getting beaten up again, when really I did care. I was an emotional wreck. I'd find myself doing things like missing the last train from London and sleeping rough with a bunch of crack addicts, and a boy prostitute, who helped me out for a time, but when he needed his next fix he nicked off with all the money I had. And I start to wonder – did I create this shit to have something to do, to think about, to talk about? At least misery can cut through the numb and endless boredom; conflict can validate and bring life to any dull existence. Have I all this time been picking away at myself, killing myself little by little, because I haven't got the guts to get it over with in one fell swoop?

Back in my hospital bed I am surrounded by papers and pens, desperately trying to document my downfall, to make sense of it all, to account for this life's filtering out, clinging on to desperate strands. The nurses wonder why I'm writing and drawing – *"It will put too much of a strain on your mind"* – they say. I really don't know why myself. From the perspective of this sickness my creative ego seems absurd. Why do I perform these strange dances? Why do I document this sinking ship? For sentiment? To leave a legacy? Why did the cameraman keep filming when the Hindenburg went up in flames? My downfall isn't nearly as spectacular.

Perhaps all along I *was* subconsciously constructing elaborate plans for my own death; the greatest show…

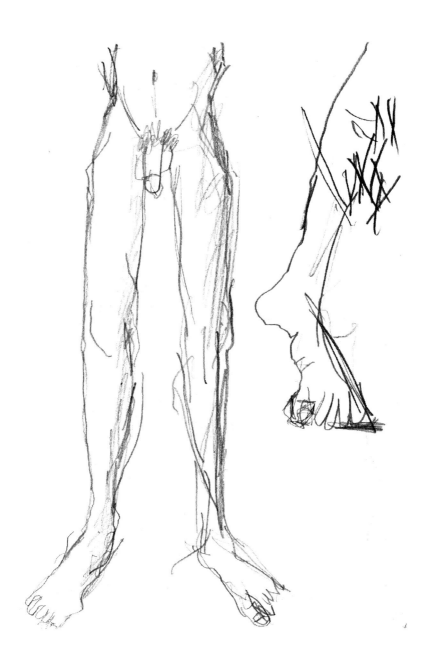

FEEL A GOOD BIT BETTER NOW

FROM MY HOSPITAL BED,
DON'T EXPECT ME TO
PAINT A LANDSCAPE

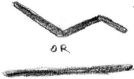 OR

THE BED IS ADJUSTABLE
I MUSTN'T LEAVE
THE ROOM

"I GOT THE TB BLUES"
(I THINK IT WAS LEADBELLY)

Duke's Mound was the hardest of the three stories to put onto paper, as I was fictionalising events as they were occurring with no real idea of the outcome.

Initially, after the best part of a year back in Hastings – gradually piecing my ego back together, as well as putting the flesh back on my bones and the strength into my limbs – I found myself spending increasingly more time in London, where my closest friends were living. Among them were Alex and Salena, who had separately and in their own different ways already provided the inspiration for what was to become the character Epiphany.

My first few attempts at resuming my previous levels of drug consumption had resulted in much vomiting and the coughing up of great globs of phlegm; the aftermath of the tuberculosis had not yet fully left my lungs, and one of them was still housing a swollen lymph node the size of an avocado. I was also regularly incontinent, so was back on the sanitary towels again.

Having declined the offer to return to university (I was glad to have an excuse to leave), I decided that the best thing for me to do was to create a new beginning. My immune system could no longer stand the pollution and excessive drug use it had endured when living in London, nor could my weakened self-esteem endure the prevailing narrow-mindedness of Hastings. Moving abroad would have been unwise for matters of finance and family support. So it seemed there was only one solution: I would move to Brighton.

Not long after the move I found myself in what was (to begin with) the first sensible, monogamous and mutually caring relationship I had experienced. From the moment I met him, Ben, my new boyfriend, had provided me with stability and absolute support for my creativity. So he was naturally supportive when I told him that I was in the process of writing three stories of varying autobiographical content, the last of which I had not finished yet, but which was to be about us.

As my mental state post-illness had been in constant fluctuation between the life-affirming joy of realising that I could easily have died and a crushing awareness of the futility of existence, I was curious to explore the nature of my tendencies towards self-destruction. Perhaps my selfish desire for authenticity had caused me to be somewhat negligent of the inherent dangers in creating a self-fulfilling prophecy.

The truth is more painful.

*   *   *

DUKE'S MOUND

*   *   *

'There is no redemption without sin. That is, at least with sin there is a journey. When we do something we later get a guilty conscience about, something we construe as bad, we are put in contact with our belief system and a journey takes place. This journey of self-analysis is a catalyst for progression. A relationship can often bear more fruit with something to potentially jeopardise it; conflict can strengthen an emotional bond. Some relationships thrive on conflict, or a power struggle, as a catalyst, or else they peter out into emotional nothingness and the love is lost …There is no redemption without sin …there is no redemption without sin.'

*   *   *

In Cameron, Richard had found something he had never before experienced. He was hesitant to use frivolous words such as love, but what he felt when their bodies interlocked, when their fluids intermingled on Cameron's bed linen on which they slept, when he and Cameron shared saliva, passed oxygen from one lung to another until it was just carbon dioxide, when their bodies slotted together and their hearts beat in unison, Richard was no longer alone. What he felt was true emotion, pure joy, not a drug or the mere stimulation of his loins. It was as if the great emotional wound he had always lived with was now starting to heal. There was still a niggling cynicism at the back of his mind that perhaps what he was feeling was just delusional, a rush of chemicals from experiencing his first *real* emotional human contact – someone who was fully prepared to take him on board for all his complications, his issues and failings. *'What good is it to place meaning on emotions, other than to maintain a contented self-deception?'* – thought Richard – the cynical part of his mind still wanting to hold back, still niggling away – *'You're making sandcastles out of shit – it will all fall down in time, it always does.'* That self-destructive voice in the back of Richard's mind telling him he's going to fuck it up – *'anything you've ever had that's any good slips through your hands. This won't last for long.'* Perhaps, but for now this voice was a mere whisper engulfed by the good he was feeling, and in time Richard hoped he could suffocate this voice fully with all the love he felt – yes, perhaps it *was* love he was feeling.

∗   ∗   ∗

The guy has Richard in a corner of the temple area, looming powerfully over him. *"So mate, what you into?"* – his voice gruff and deep. Richard has already pocketed a few packets of condoms from the box left by the street outreach people – *"I like getting fucked"* – Richard trying to sound hard, dressed in a baseball cap, Nike hoodie, and adidas tracksuit bottoms and trainers. Not his regular attire – Richard had a kind of fetish for average, sporty clothing, though he had no interest in sports. This ensemble was reserved exclusively for sexual encounters, and had been lying at the bottom of a cupboard for the two months he had been with Cameron. The clothes turned him on and made him feel hard; they also made him look inconspicuous, so if anyone he knew were to wander down here, chances are that Richard would notice them first.

The man reaches forward to grope Richard's balls and cock, which show hard through his tracksuit bottoms – *"Yeeah, you got some fuckin' nice cock on you boy. You into fucking as well?"* At that moment all Richard wanted was to be dominated – *really* dominated – to feel powerless, to experience again those mixed sensations of pleasure and pain. From being broken in the first few times, the rough experiences in the toilets, Richard was used to being degraded, being dominated. He felt that degradation suited him. At times it was as if it burned a hole to his conscious mind, that *that* was all he was about, he *deserved* to be treated badly, he *deserved* to be degraded. It had always been there, niggling away at the back of his mind, through all the good times with Cameron; his mother now feeling happy for him, happy that he had someone who loved him, happy he was happy. Somewhere Richard had always known he would fuck it up. He could never live up to the expectations of his mother and his family, and he didn't deserve Cameron's love. In Richard's mind at that moment, he knew, he was just a filthy perv; always had been – a worthless faggot who deserved all the shit he got.

"I want you to fuck me man. I like to be dominated" – Richard's voice wavering slightly as his heartbeat palpitates. *"Yeah, you like a bit of rough, do you, you filthy slut?"* – pushing Richard against the wall as he spits on him – *"you like that, you filthy*

cunt?" – *"Yeah"* – blinking the gob from his eye, phlegm running down his cheek and dripping in globs from his chin. *"You wanna be fucked then?"* Turning him around, the man forces his weight upon him, pushing him down into the piss-stained corner. With one hand he pushes a bottle of poppers under Richard's nose, his other hand down the back of his pants, his thick index finger working its way, dry, up Richard's arse – *"You into scat boy?"* – *"…What?"* …something to do with jazz music, he thinks, confused, his pulse inflating with the poppers swelling his wasted brain – *"err …yeah."* The guy withdraws his shit-stained finger and shoves it in Richard's mouth – gagging – *"not that man …I'm not into that…"*

By now, all the other men in the temple area have cottoned on that Richard and this other guy are the horniest thing going on in the place. Gathering around they try to muscle in on the action. An unattractive older man attempts to position himself behind Richard's exposed buttocks. *"We should go into the bushes"* – Richard's dominator roughly pushing away the old guy who is trying to shove his cock up Richard's arse.

Following the man down the lamplit path, Richard looks at the dark hairs on his hard callused hands. Richard had always liked a man with big hands, hands that he could be crushed by, hands that made him feel weak. Turning a sharp right into the bushes, the man – pushing aside the leaves and branches with his strong arms – looks back at Richard, gesturing for him to follow…

…In the darkness, Richard can feel his tracksuit bottoms being loosened and those large hands reaching in, dry and warm, to free his aching cock. The man feeling underneath Richard's sweaty crotch, then with one finger up Richard's arse, his other arm around his waist, hoisting him up and lowering him into the dirt. Richard's face pressed into the dirt, his arse sticking up into the air; the guy slapping Richard's arse hard, the sting subsiding to a warm glow – *"You like that?"* – *"Yeah man, fuck me – please fuck me."* The man lifting back Richard's head and pressing the poppers bottle against his nose; Richard again feeling the surge to his brain through his neck; his heart and arteries all pulsating. The guy forcing Richard's face back into the dirt; spitting on his arse and working a finger in. Richard's mind still pulsating; intending to reach for the condom pack in his pocket, but so taken by the sensations he doesn't bother. His head is again lifted out of the dirt; more poppers that spill onto his top lip, all the molecules evaporating with a mild burning sensation. The wave that follows so encompasses Richard that he hardly notices the man's unsheathed cock enter him – the sensation is so great ...he doesn't care.

Time abstracted into waves of pleasure and disorientation – Richard's sphincter dilating and contracting with every thrust. Sometimes the man's cock exits completely then plunges home with deft accuracy; sometimes the thrusts slow and the man lowers his weight on, around, inside Richard. His stubble scraping on Richard's cheek as he whispers – *"You into fisting?"* Richard's head has cleared slightly – *"I don't think I could"* – *"You've got a good arse on you ...with a bit of training you could."* Again pushing the poppers bottle under Richard's nose, spilling more than the previous time; Richard's top lip feeling sore, but as the wave engulfs him he soon forgets. Feeling the hand around his cock and balls again; the man withdrawing himself and hoisting Richard's arse up out of the dirt, where his whole body had been pressed – *"You got some lube?"* Richard fumbling for the condom packet that he *should* have reached for a half-hour ago, the thumping in his brain intensifying. He can hear the man behind his spread cheeks tearing open the packet of lube; he can feel the thick tough fingers work a little up his arsehole – first one, then two, screwing him as he rotates his wrist from side to side; three fingers; Richard inhaling sharply, filling his lungs with more poppers; four fingers, working from side to side – *"That's it boy, relax, you can take it."* Richard is aware that his own penis is not erect. The pleasure he is deriving from this experience is not merely sexual, it is reaffirming the pain he had felt those first few times; he is being broken in, being stretched from the inside out, the sensation filling his whole being. For all the agony, the taste of dirt, the sheer weight upon him, working its way inside him, Richard knows he is alive. The guy fitting in his thumb, thrusting rhythmically, though not hard enough to enter beyond his knuckles. Now Richard is really feeling it, his eyes watering – *"Ohh Jeeesus-stop-no, don't stop-oh pleease-fuck...yeah...oh-no"* – the pain increasing; feeling as if he could split in two as the knuckles of the hand reach his well-dilated muscle – *"ohhh...stop...yes...no-STOP-STOP!!"* The man stops – *"Are you sure? I nearly had it in all the way."* Richard is coming to his senses again, his mind slowly clearing, pulse slowing – *"Yeah, that was great man, but ...yeah, it had to stop"* – *"But I was nearly in all the way ...fuck, you're dirty."* Richard – now aware that the backs of his thighs are awash with his own excrement – salvages a disintegrating tissue from his pocket and wipes up as best he can, accidentally caking his hands in his own shit. *"The dew on these leaves will clean off your hands"* – the man, rubbing the leaves between his hands. Richard, finding this works, dries his hands on his tracksuit bottoms. The insides are caked in shit anyway – all his clothes will have to be thoroughly washed.

Making his excuses, Richard walks the long sore walk home, his tracksuit bottoms sticking to his drying legs, the niggling voice ringing in his mind – *'I told you you'd fuck it up.'* Observing his hands, where the shit has dried, under his nails and between his fingers – it now looks like harmless mud. He must not let Cameron know what he has done; he must wash it all away.

∗　　　∗　　　∗

The decision to move to Brighton had been sudden, but Richard's parents were very supportive. They had seen the cuts on his arms, his half-arsed cries for help, and though they still hoped that someday he might have a wife and give them grandchildren, they reacted well when he told them that he was gay, and put it to the back of their minds. *'Young people often question themselves'* – his mother thought – *'...even that David Bowie has a wife now.'* They respected his decision to move to Brighton, and could see that his outlook on life had already improved with this as a goal. They helped him find a bedsit room, and, with the money he had inherited from the death of his grandfather, he was able to pay the deposit plus the first couple of months' rent, and still have a few hundred left until he could find a job.

He had met Cameron in a bar. Not used to socialising without a head full of speed, Richard knew no dealers in Brighton, so decided to make a concerted effort at a fresh start. Cameron was the same height as Richard, but three years older; wise-looking and softly spoken. Richard had approached *him* (something he was not used to doing), to ask for a cigarette. As those first days in Brighton passed, Richard would often meet Cameron, and as they talked Richard found that Cameron had shared similar sexual experiences in his youth – *"Your first sexual experiences do shape you,"* he'd said. A real bond developed between them, and they both agreed they would do all that they could to be true to one another.

Cameron had become the stabilising influence Richard needed, the relationship he had always aspired to but never found. Of course he had fucked up that one time, but any feelings of guilt could easily be overridden by the thought that – *'If Cameron hadn't told me about the place I would never have gone.'* Richard's fascination with the place had grown daily for those first two months of their relationship. He had always known that in time he would visit the area, be it from curiosity or the sheer defiance of that part of his mind that wanted to disrupt anything good he had, throwing up chaos to jeopardise his stability. He had been to the place, so surely now his curiosity was sated. After all, he had promised to make an effort to remain committed; what he had created with Cameron was far too good to lose. Cameron worked all day, so it was no problem for Richard to sort out an appointment at the clinic without raising any suspicion. It was important he got himself checked out.

Taking his ticket stub from the dispenser on the wall, Richard finds a seat. On his arrival he had noted, with some humour, that the STD clinic is situated only a short walk from the cruising ground.

The wait in such sterile surroundings always seems long and drawn out – nothing to look at but women's trivia magazines or the face of the person opposite. Running his tongue along the inside of his cheek, Richard feels the flesh on which he used to gnaw over many long days and nights of amphetamine and pills. It has now healed to form a line of scar tissue. It seems that all his wounds are now healing – leaving him somewhat callused and scarred, but no longer an open wound for anyone to fuck over. Cameron is good for him – everything he needs; he will get himself checked out by the doctor and then he will be able to put the whole thing behind him. Richard reclines in his seat, head back, basking in the memory of Cameron's smile, till a buzzing sound breaks his silence and he realises his number has been called.

The doctor claps a warm hand around Richard's and gives it a firm shake – *"Good morning, young sir, and how may I help you?"* Releasing his grip, the ruddy-cheeked doctor turns to his desk, gesturing for Richard to sit. *"...Now let's see... Richard Eastwood..."* – flicking through Richard's records – *"what seems to be the trouble?"* – *"I just thought I ought to get myself checked out. I had some unprotected sex and I wouldn't want to pass anything on to my boyfriend"* – *"...Okay, so I'm assuming it was another male who you had unprotected sex with?"* – *"...Yes"* – *"...And when was this?"* – *"...Three days ago."* The doctor turns to Richard's file and makes notes – *"...And were you the active or passive party?"* – *"...Passive"* – *"...Very well ...of course, you realise that you stand a higher chance of having had any virus or infection passed onto you if you were the passive party, and if you have had another man's come inside you ...I'll get the nurse to take your bloods but first I'll examine you and take some swabs. If you'd care to strip – just your bottom half will do ...and then if you'd lie on your side on the couch with your back to me ...if that's okay?"*

...The doctor's mannerisms are comforting and Richard doesn't feel degraded by having to strip off in such sterile surroundings. The doctor stretches a wide reel of blue tissue paper across the couch and Richard reclines facing the wall. The latex glove is cold as the doctor lubricates and probes – *"Yes, it seems there could possibly be some kind of discharge"* – a swab is gently inserted, the cold gloves parting Richard's cheeks ...Richard staring at the wall just inches from his face, trying not to think of anything but unable to shake the image of his mother from his mind – *'What would she be thinking if she could see me now?'* – *"...Now if you could just lie on your back so I can get a good look at your penis..."* Richard turns and the doctor lifts and pulls back the skin, squeezing at the base and pulling his hand up as if trying to milk the wilted cock – *"...have you been experiencing any problems when passing water – a burning sensation, for instance?"* – *"Ummm"* – Richard pausing to think, distracted by the sensation of the hand around his cock – *"not that I can think of"* – feeling a rush of arousal ...trying to force it back ...trying to regain the image of his mother ...doctor milks and examines ...Richard feeling a swell of blood to his penis ...unable to control ...getting gradually harder ...doctor still gently milking ...examining ...milking ...examining. *"I'm sorry"* – Richard, deeply embarrassed at his now full erection – *"sometimes it seems to have a life of its own"* – *"Most interesting"* – the doctor taking a fresh swab from its plastic container – *"this is likely to sting a little"* – inserting it into Richard's urethra and twisting gently as Richard winces in pain, then removing it and putting it back into its labelled container to be sent to the laboratory – *"...do you know why it does that?"* – the doctor looking with some curiosity at Richard's penis. *"I'm not sure ...I've just always had a very high sex drive"* – *"Well, that's certainly very healthy for a boy of your age"* – the doctor lifting back the erect cock, examining Richard's balls, rolling them between thumb and forefinger ...Richard trying not to make eye contact ...trying again to visualise his mother; the image forced out of his mind by that of the man on top of him in the bushes, pushing his face into the dirt; this image in stark contrast with the sterility of his present surroundings; the white latex-gloved hand back around his cock, gently milking and examining – *"of course, for some people it's a turn-on to be examined like this"* – *"...Oh, yes, I suppose so"* – trying not to sound too interested, thinking of his mother, thinking of Cameron, getting an image in his mind of his mother and Cameron fucking, then quickly blinking it out, repulsed at the thought; that he had conjured it up. The doctor seems to be holding Richard's cock for an abnormally long time. He looks up at Richard, and, on seeing his averted eyes, coughs nervously and moves his hand away – *"Okay, that should be enough. If you'd like to put your clothes on"* – the doctor seems somewhat nervous; his pace has gathered slightly. He returns to his desk as Richard pulls his pants and trousers up and puts on his shoes, pushing his awkward but now decreasing erection upwards so it is held in place by the elastic of his boxer shorts. *"...So ...if you would go to the nurse for bloods and make an appointment for three months' time, we'll contact you if anything is wrong"* – again shaking Richard's hand and giving him a knowing smile – *"I shall look forward to seeing you again."* Richard averting his eyes, still embarrassed – *"hopefully not too soon"* – *"Of course"* – the doctor's smile glazing slightly. He gives Richard a nod and opens the door. *"Good-bye"* – says Richard. *"See you"* – replies the doctor.

∗   ∗   ∗

It's another two hours before Cameron is to return from work. The familiar, albeit mild, sensation of debasement that Richard had again experienced – this time at the hands of his doctor – has caused in him a strange shift: as if a kind of magnetism is willing him back to the area where he had had his experience. Richard quickly turning this impulse into a conscious intention – *'To see the grounds by the light of day would demystify them'* – he thinks – *' I have no intention to go there again for sex.'* Still, an emotive mixture of curiosity and repulsion simmers in his gut as he turns from his intended path, deviating towards the seafront and the Mound.

By the harsh light of day the place looks unthreatening – a parkland area on the incline of a slope; alcoves for benches and areas of bush and shrubbery. There are a few men cruising, most of whom look at least twice Richard's age and not the type he would normally be attracted to. They walk briskly, seeming to mind their own business as their paths cross that of a dog walker, or some kids from the nearby skate park. Richard walks the path to the central temple area, a large concrete construction, partly concealed among the bushes. The odour of penetrated rectum hangs heavy in the air, mingling with the smell of stagnant urine that Richard associates with his formative experiences in the toilets of Robertsfield. Scuffing his feet through the litter of torn condoms, he can hear groans from a couple screwing in the adjacent chamber. Though mildly aroused he does not feel inclined to look, instead making his way to the bushes in which *he* had been so roughly screwed.

Looking at the ground, Richard imagines he can see the outline of the place where his body had been pressed into the dirt. He feels very little – cold and detached; he had hoped that this visit would put some of his demons to rest, but inside it feels like little has changed.

A fresh breeze hits him as he descends to the seafront and towards Cameron's house. Richard observing how the wind has stretched the clouds across the sky to catch the glowing orange of the sun. With a deep inhalation of fresh sea air, he feels a rare wave of optimism – *'It's not too late for me and Cameron'* – reaching into his pocket for his wallet.

*   *   *

Sweeping past Cameron into the living room, clutching an oversized carrier bag in his arms. *"Whoa! You're excitable today"* – Cameron, glad to see his handsome boy in such high spirits – *"what's in the bag?"* – *"...Things, I got you good things"* – reaching into the bag – *"...a duck, a whole dead duck – I know you like duck"* – *"But you can't afford..."* –

"...I went to the supermarket and bought a duck, some asparagus, king prawns, avocado, baby spinach, smoked salmon ...good food... I wanted to make you something memorable" – *"And what are you going to make with all that?"* – *"I'll improvise"* – and Richard and Cameron – holding each other – kiss and talk of the notion of love; that Richard had thought he would never know what the word meant, but if ever he did he was feeling it now. Then preparing a salad and roasting the duck as Cameron skins up. They smoke, and the food tastes *so* good and they eat at the thought of each other, and afterwards as Richard lies in Cameron's arms, glowing in his warmth, he gets up with a start as he has forgotten Cameron's *real* gift, and taking a silver ring from his pocket – *"This is for you – I'm not saying we're married or anything, but I wanted you to have something personal to wear."* And Cameron saying nothing – so touched by the gift – instead holds Richard closer, and Richard holds him, and they kiss and they kiss until, copulating ecstatic, they roll off the sofa and across the living room floor.

* * *

Not wanting to disturb Richard as he gets up for work, Cameron dresses quietly as he often does, preparing himself a cup of coffee before gently kissing his lover on the cheek. When Richard wakes it is 10:30. He rolls over to Cameron's side of the bed, and, noticing him gone, stretches out, warm with the glow of the previous evening. Pulling all of the pillows close to him, he wraps his legs around them, imagining it is Cameron's body. He misses not being able to lie in with Cameron on weekdays.

Deciding he'll make something of his day, Richard heads into town. He had been in Brighton three months and hadn't really seen much of the town, except for the job centre, a couple of gay bars and the cruising ground. Taking a walk through the

Lanes and past the Pavilion, Richard admires its vast bulbous domes – *'A perfect landmark for Brighton ...I couldn't imagine a camper building.'* Settling beneath the iron girders of the pier he looks out to sea, breathing in the fresh September air, the first smells of autumn. As he lies back on one of the pier's vast supports he smiles inwardly – *'This is a place to be truly free'* ...Richard *feeling* this to be true, not only within himself but in the expressions of people walking by, devoid of the confrontational defensiveness that the people of Robertsfield seemed to have – *'...I could never have asked for anything more ...I can really be myself here'* – and as the warmth he is feeling intensifies, he closes his eyes and lets it consume him ...Until he is awakened by the waves, lapping at his feet. So Richard, enriched with positive emotion and inspiration, heads for his bedsit room to paint and create, leaving the job centre to another day – *'this feeling is too good to waste.'*

*   *   *

As the autumn sets in, Richard and Cameron are glad to have each other for warmth and comfort. In past years this time of year has seemed to drag, but now the days and weeks just drift by. Though Cameron has cut him a key to his flat, Richard still spends the weekdays in his bedsit room, painting and writing poetry, as well as going to the job centre once a week to blag his way to the next giro. He is immersed in a great dynamic painting on a door that he found in the street when his mobile rings. *"...Hello, Richard?"* – *"...Yes."* The voice on the other end sounds familiar, but Richard is unable to put his finger on it. *"...This is Doctor Goldsmith, from the clinic. I was wondering if you shouldn't come in so we can discuss your results and give you another check over..."* – *"...Sure, okay ...if you think I should"* – Richard feeling concerned,

87

but deciding not to worry until he knows anything for certain. *"...Is today alright for you?"* – *"...Yeah, whenever's fine"* – *"...Four o'clock then?"* – *"...Okay"* – *"...Good then, I'll see you at four."* Richard puts down the phone, slightly puzzled that his doctor should phone him in person, instead of through his secretary. But he shrugs it off and returns to his artwork.

*   *   *

Arriving at the clinic just after four, Richard, expecting the usual long wait, has been sitting for barely two minutes when he is called to the desk – *"Mr Eastwood? The doctor is ready to see you now."* At first quite taken aback at the speed at which he is being seen, Richard makes his way down the long corridor to the doctor's consulting room.

The grin that greets him fills the room; again the doctor envelops Richard's hand in his – *"Richard! How have you been keeping? ...Eating well I hope"* – *"Yes, my boyfriend and I..."* – *"...Marvellous to hear. Do take a seat"* – as the doctor opens Richard's records and examines the coloured papers – *"well, we've got your results back and everything seems to be fine. Though I do think a general examination would be in order ...and then you can be on your way."* Feeling slightly bemused, then beginning to suspect that the doctor has an ulterior motive in asking him here, Richard feels shock at first, before experiencing an uninvited rush of arousal – *"Yes, but I haven't been sleeping around since the last time I was here."* The doctor looking at Richard with a raised eyebrow – *"Do you ever check yourself for lumps? ...There are also other complaints, such as genital warts, which may take longer to surface ...now if you wouldn't mind"* – as the doctor gestures to the couch; and Richard, lowering his pants and trousers (and noticing the doctor pull the blind shut and bolt the door), again fights back the swell of arousal to his penis. It isn't even as if he finds the doctor attractive. He seems a rather well-rounded man, probably in his mid to late thirties, with ruddy cheeks and thinning on top. Richard puts back his head, trying to stay calm as the doctor caresses his genitals. He knows his cock is now erect, but doesn't want to look, feeling the movements of the doctor's hand (more sensual than before) over his balls and around the shaft of his penis. Richard, feeling an unusual sensation on the tip of his penis, looks down for a moment, and sees that it is dewed with pre-come; the doctor gently blowing warm air on the helmet, before removing the pearl of jism with his gloved hand. *"Will that be enough?"* – Richard's voice jarring from his nerves; the doctor smiling, embarrassed – *"Oh ...oh yes, I'm sure everything's in order"* – as he takes off his latex gloves and pauses for a moment, his hands hovering with the gloves above the clinical waste bin, before placing them carefully to one side.

*　　　*　　　*

On leaving the clinic, Richard again feels the impulse to walk to the Mound. What the doctor did has reawoken in Richard a familiar voice, the voice of desire that he had long been struggling to repress. He enjoyed how it had felt, the rush of danger, the feel of another man's hand on his cock (recently Cameron's hand and body had felt no different from his own; the extremes of emotion they had felt for one another also seemed to be merging into a mutually secure, though equally predictable, blob). The once-suppressed voice that often recognised that Richard would come back to his old routines was now starting to settle comfortably in his head – *'You're a fucking homosexual, for Christ's sake – you're not supposed to be monogamous'* – Richard beginning to feel sated at the acceptance of this notion – *'you wanted the doctor to follow through – you loved it; that's all you've ever been about... when was the last time you got right off your head and did something really fucked up?'* Richard, taking his tobacco pouch from his pocket, feels for his lump of hash – there seems to be the best part of an eighth left, and Cameron still has some at home. Biting at a corner, a sizable chunk breaks off in his mouth, which he nibbles into smaller pieces with his front teeth before swallowing the resulting grit. It is gone five-thirty and already dark (though surprisingly mild for the time of year). Now at a crossroads, Richard hovers painfully for a moment, aware that his will is weak but feeling increasingly happy to submit to this weakness. Reaching for his mobile phone he presses Cameron's number, quite sure that he will not be home from work yet. The phone rings a few times before clicking onto the answering machine – *"Oh, hi monkey, it's just me... I'm calling to say that something's come up and I won't be home tonight"* – *'Sure something's come up: your fucking erection'* – *"...I love you and I'll see you tomorrow"* – turning his mobile phone off and putting it into his pocket, then biting off another lump of hash and tingling with excitement and anticipation as he takes the first steps towards the place... *'Yeah, that's right ...I knew you would.'*

*   *   *

In the hollow darkness of the bushes there is no sound. Only the muffled fumblings of cock on cock, the occasional grunt between tentative hungry breaths. Then suddenly a FLASH and sizzzzle-burning-fuze breaks white into the darkness; shot into the cruisers' midst it cracks open with a BANG! Richard, recoiling in stoned paranoia, quickly withdraws his cock from some guy's mouth; the sudden jerk causing his helmet to snag on the guy's teeth. With his heartbeat racing from shock he hurriedly shoves his grazed dick back into his pants, positioning himself towards the direction of the attack. FLASH-another-hissssss-incendiaryshot-and-BANG! This

90

time the explosion is in the path of a middle-aged man. He continues on his path seemingly unperturbed. It seems some kids are camped out on the lawn at the bottom of the bushes and are catapulting bangers at the cruisers.

Deciding to make a move to the uppermost level of the cruising ground, Richard exits the main chamber, attempting to look casual as he walks along one of the more exposed pathways. He can hear the voices of the kids on the grass below him to his right, their laughter ringing in his paranoid head (by this point he has consumed orally the best part of the eighth; the depth of his intoxication now bordering on tripping). He hears a stone bounce off a metal post to his left. Keeping his head down, casual, he continues forward, increasing pace a little, but not too obviously. Heading up some steps and around the corner, he enters the uppermost and most exposed area of the cruising ground. Noticing voices and sniggering from the high wall by the main road that overlooks the bushes, he looks to see several groups of three or four men, peering over the wall, making comments, pointing and laughing. A kid walks by and looks at Richard with what he construes as disgust.

This is when real paranoia sets in – '*It seems that all the straight people are onto our game and may have invaded our midst*' – Richard is unable to tell if the people he sees around him are genuine cruisers, or men trying to lure a *real* fag, to do some serious harm to – '*Get him in a dark corner with his pants down and castrate the fucker – thrust the blade into the flesh of his torn scrotum-sack and twist it round some, before you cut the faggot's throat and leave him there – the copper taste filling his mouth – his lungs inhaling only blood now – warmly pumping into the dirt as his heart-beat—slows—and— —stops.*' – '*...Fuck man, it could be me! I should just go home now*' – the sensible part of Richard's mind coming to the forefront for a moment, only to be overridden by his cock and curiosity. Richard looking each guy in the eye: *queer? Impostor?* For most it's hard to tell ...some are blatantly queer, others less obvious. Walking full circle he returns to the temple area in the centre of the grounds. In the darkness he scours the corners, in fear of nail bombs; unattended bags. Seeing men groping and fucking, oblivious to what is going on outside. His paranoia extending to the notion that perhaps these men are straight men (right wing extremists) miming sexual acts in the darkness so their well-planned attack won't be suspected until it's too late – *'Out with the baseball bats and cut-throat razors.'* – *'...Fuck – my mind is playing up. Should I call the police? ...Should I ask one of these guys if they think something weird is going on? What if I do and I find I'm speaking to one of the enemy? Who can I trust?'*

Richard decides to exit the chamber in the same direction as before – the bushes are darker here, faces are less easily distinguishable. He can still hear the kids camping out on the grass, but they seem to have calmed somewhat. Two guys stand in the half-dark – he makes eye contact with one of them, who pouts his lips into a kissy face. Instantly freaked out, Richard hurriedly passes (genuine cruisers tend to work on eye contact alone; perhaps the occasional smile. This pursed-lips-kiss gesture seems to Richard to be a straight man's idea of what gay men do as a come-on. It seems an intentionally camp gesture – a real gay man would be far more subtle). He can hear the men following him.

In his creeping terror, blood pressure rising, pulse increasing, he decides to head for home. Walking down the low road parallel with the sea he can see the lights of an approaching vehicle. As it comes nearer it slows but doesn't stop, cruising past with dark imposing windows. It is a police van. Richard can sense that they are observing him. A shiver runs the length of his spine as he feels a million invisible eyes penetrate his tired and paranoid mind.

Quick! To home, to sleep, with dreams of nothing but the frightened waltz from cock to cock …insatiable desires never to be fulfilled as he walks an endless spiral in the hateful-hollow-dark.

*   *   *

'…I'd arranged to meet someone and I just forgot to call …no, that won't work – he knows I don't know anyone here. Okay… I was feeling sick and I just wanted some time to myself …but I'd want him around if I was ill … I'd at least call him' – "FUCK!" – pacing up and down on the pavement just around the corner from Cameron's flat – *'I know! …A friend was visiting from Robertsfield and we just got completely trashed …that'll do – but who? Epiphany I guess …he'll wonder why I didn't invite her round …oh bollocks!'* Turning the corner and swallowing back his guilt as he reaches for the doorbell.

"Hello…" – Cameron managing to sound both surprised and questioning, whilst playing down any undertones of suspicion – *"where were you last night? I couldn't get hold of you."* Slowly feeling his intentions weaken under Cameron's inquiring gaze, Richard kisses him (avoiding direct eye contact) and passes into the living room. Seating himself, Richard cringes inside as he takes a deep breath, unable to sustain his pretence – *"…I've been fucking around …I'm sorry."* Cameron remaining silent, evidently hurt. *"I just can't seem to get the impulse for random sex out of my mind …I guess it was rammed into me from a young age …bad joke, I know …I'm sorry"* – looking desperately to Cameron for a response – *"…please say something… I've told you I'm sorry …you know you're the best thing that's happened to me"* –

93

tears welling in Richard's eyes – *"...Cameron?"* Cameron staring blankly at the floor, a pained expression on his face. After what seems an eternity he takes a breath to speak – *"...You know, I understand you – I was just the same ...I guess it's different 'cause I'm that much older ...it might take me time to get used to it, though ...it does upset me to think of you..."* – sighing – *"...I had my suspicions."* Cameron opens his arms to Richard and they embrace, but somehow something seems to be missing. Later, in bed, they don't have sex, and Richard – lying by Cameron's side, wanting to reach over and embrace him – feels distanced by his guilt. So instead of reaching out, he sinks deeper inside the cold isolation of himself.

*   *   *

Richard had intended to paint the following day, but somehow didn't feel inspired. It was only when Cameron phoned him after work that he started to relax and feel the weight lift from him. *"I've been thinking..."* – Cameron's voice sounding mischievously buoyant – *"...I reckon I'd have a problem with watching someone else fuck you ...but seeing as we've both had sex in the past with pretty rough-looking older men, wouldn't it be cool if one time we took control?"* – *"...What did you have in mind?"* – Richard confused, his curiosity growing. *"...I thought – what if we picked up a pervy old man and played the dominator with him? ... It could be cathartic. What do you think?"* Richard warming to the idea – *"Sounds like a laugh... what made you think of..."* – *"Oh, I just thought maybe I'm too uptight; we should experiment more"* – pausing for a moment in thought – *"...besides, I'd probably get jealous if we had a threesome with a younger guy."*

Four hours and the best part of a litre bottle of whisky later, Richard and Cameron find themselves in a seedy bar with a pretty rough-looking (though somewhat handsome through the drunken haze of their minds) alcoholic in his late forties. They had clocked him simultaneously: he had the look of an ex-boxer turned drunk, and must have been very attractive in his youth; now brought down a notch or two by his swollen beer gut and blotched complexion – *I thought I saw you boys looking at me...* – swaying as he leers drunkenly over where they are seated – *"...I just want to say I think you're fuuukin beautiful..."*

...That was all it took. Within the hour he's hog-tied on Cameron's living room floor, his butt up in the air, and Cameron working the neck of a wine bottle up it and laughing. *"You boys are pretty fucked up..."* – the man sweating and straining with discomfort, though evidently enjoying the degradation, and Richard, aware of his swelling bladder – *"What say we piss on this fucker?"* – then him and Cameron towering over the crumpled blob on the floor and letting flow, getting off on watching the guy squirm, too pissed to care about saturating the worn carpet. Richard takes a swig from the last of the whisky and passes it to Cameron, before slumping exhausted on the dampness of the floor and – laughing – rolls over onto his front, his ass in the air, and Cameron untying the guy – now drenched in piss and sweat, saturating the dark hairs that cover his sagging breasts and swollen gut: the guy pointing at Richard's arse – *I'd really love a piece of that."* And Richard rolling drunkenly, butt up in the air, loving the admiration, so Cameron ensuring that the man wears a condom, and Richard now asking to be tied up, giving himself up to the idea of total helpless degradation (and Cameron can't get jealous as the guy is blatantly rough-looking); but Cameron – now starting to have doubts, and feeling awkward about the situation; feeling left out – though not wishing to participate – as he watches the man pumping

95

into the oblivious Richard until reaching his climax and withdrawing, and as Cameron unties Richard they're both thinking that maybe they should have finished with degrading the man with the wine bottle and then asked him to leave. Cameron hands him his clothes but the guy's just sitting there smiling and stroking Richard's arse. *"Yeah, I think it's time to go now!"* – Cameron trying to sound authoritative; the man seeming to take as much time as possible to put each sock on; every item of clothing seeming to take an eternity, as Cameron feels the stress slowly welling up inside him until, as they finally shut the door behind the guy, he feels as if he is about to burst with his welling rage and bitter sadness – *"I couldn't take seeing that guy fuck you"* – looking with disgust at the sodden carpet – *"...I just can't stand thinking of you with anyone else."* Richard detecting the bitterness in Cameron's voice and reacting with a cold detachment – *"It was your idea that we picked up the man ...it's not like I'm going to run off with him or anything"* – slurring from too much whisky – *"I can't believe you're fucking jealous!"* Cameron's sadness turning to anger at the accusation – *"IS IT TOO MUCH TO ASK THAT I DON'T HAVE TO WORRY ABOUT WHAT MY BOYFRIEND IS DOING?"* Richard swigging back the dregs of the whisky with a casual contempt at Cameron's outburst. *"OR THAT HE'S EVEN GOING TO COME HOME AT ALL, 'CAUSE HE'S TOO BUSY GETTING HIS ARSE FUCKED BY SOME FUCKING STRANGER!?"* ...Richard finding his own anger and bitterness twist inside him – *"FUCK YOU ...YOU DON'T OWN MY ARSE"* – and heading for the door as the emotions wrench at his core, half-aware somewhere that the anger he is feeling shouldn't really be directed at Cameron – it is anger he feels at himself and his inability to control his lust and urges. But the overriding voice in Richard's head is forcing that knowledge down – *'Fuck him, you don't need him judging your every move'* – so still heading for the door and now opening it, hoping inside that Cameron will stop him – but Cameron is not there – and shutting the door behind him. Outside it's just the lonely night and spitting rain, and no Cameron to tell him to come back and that he's sorry…

…And Cameron sitting alone on the sofa, his feet on the piss-stained floor, hoping that Richard will change his mind and come back so they can hug and make up and everything will be okay…

*   *   *

Lying half asleep, Richard turns to his side, glad to see that Cameron is still there – *'What was that about an argument?'* He pulls himself to his feet, and, heavy with drunken tiredness, stumbles towards the toilet in slow-motion, increasingly aware in the disorientation of his half-slumber of some thick and heavy mass falling from between his legs – *'Am I shitting on Cameron's carpet?'*

Turning around, in the half light, his eyes still blurry with the static of sleep, he observes that there *is* a trail of black sticky matter leading from Cameron's bed to where he is now, standing by the toilet – *'Could my bowels be that loose?'*

Following the trail back to the bed, Richard observes that the matter seems to be odourless. He pulls back the covers of the bed, revealing, where he had lain, a giant biro the size of his arm. Not questioning the absurdity of the biro's size, Richard is sure that it must be the cause of the mess – he had been sleeping on the biro, and the black ink, as thick as tar, has leaked out onto the bed and all over his legs and lower torso.

Pulling at the sticky tar that surrounds his genitals, Richard finds it isn't coming away at all. Instead the goo is sticking to his hands and fingers as if it is multiplying in mass. Now he pulls at the tar on his hands – some comes away, taking with it chunks of surface skin, leaving his hands burning and sore.

Richard, deciding he doesn't want to employ the same technique to remove the tar from his genitals, heads for the kitchen for a pair of scissors, and starts cutting at the tar that surrounds his balls.

Then – agonising pain, as Richard realises he has cut a circular hole in the tissue of his testicles. Examining the hole, he sees it is welling up with fluid, filling his cupped hands and eventually pouring down his legs and onto the carpet. He nudges Cameron awake with his knee – *"I think I need to go to casualty!"* It is just as Cameron stirs awake that Richard wakes from *his* dream…

"…Ohhh Jesus fuuucking Christ!" – the full weight of the hangover bearing down on his frontal lobe, and noticing that he is alone in his bedsit room and that last night wasn't a dream – *"JEEESUS!"* – pulling himself to the edge of the bed, his temples throbbing, and checking his mobile – *"why won't he just phone me?"* Pulling the covers back over his head in an attempt to shut off this reality, but in need of a piss and a drink of water, though worried that any kind of excessive movement might provoke vomiting and – *'why couldn't I have just got the puking over with last night, then perhaps I wouldn't be feeling so rough now'* – *"…Oh fuck – last night; why did that have to happen?"* – and pulling himself to his feet, his mouth tasting like he's been eating sawdust, and taking tentative steps towards the toilet – *'Or should I get the water first?'* – the nausea rising from his gut and trying to swallow it down and get to the tap first, but finding it impossible to hold down, so rushing to the toilet bowl and splashing the sides some and heaving and heaving a dry and bitter rancid froth, dribbled onto the shit-stained ceramic, and still heaving,

from the pit of his gut – *'there's nothing more to come ... if only I could get to the tap'* – and the empty hollow belching subsiding for a moment, enough for Richard to make it to the sink and fill a pint glass and down it insatiably before rushing back to the toilet bowl to regurgitate the now soured water.

Pausing for a moment to get his breath, Richard sits on the seat and relieves his bladder; his bowels also empty with a desperate flump, well lubricated by the previous night's activity. Confident that the vomiting is over, he refills his pint glass and heads back to the bed, looking at the time – 11:35am – *"It's a Saturday – Cameron will be up by now; why isn't he phoning me?"* – the seconds passing by with agonising slowness, and Richard feeling a desperate welling rage – *'...Fucking cunt making me wait around for him ...he's the one with the fucking problem... I mean, does he think I enjoyed getting fucked by that disgusting old man?'* – each tick of the clock jarring frustratingly on Richard's mind, so he just wants to pick the fucking thing up and slam it against the opposite wall, but anger does no good – *'who am I angry at anyway? ...Cameron? ...Or myself, and my worthless piece of shit life'* – *"Maybe I should call him"* – *'What ...and show yourself up as the pathetic, desperate sack of shit you are? ...You haven't even got a job – what are you doing with your life?'* – the rage and bitterness subsiding for a moment – *"I know, I'll draw him a picture, or write a poem"* – reaching for the pens and paper and scribbling an image from the top of his head and looking at what he's drawn – *'It's fucking shit ...you've lost it'* – so trying instead to write a poem, but as the words come out they sound like bad cliché; Richard sickened by his own sense of inadequacy and worthlessness, so retreating again beneath the covers, and swallowing back his self-pity and his self-conscious hatred at himself and his wallowing – *'why can't I just be strong? ...Because you're weak ...because you're weak.'*

*　　　*　　　*

10:45pm – the winter wind blistering Richard's cheeks as he descends the steps to the iron archways adjacent to the sea. Keeping his distance, he observes the boy racers who are branding stripes of rubber on the tarmac below; then averting his gaze away from the lamplit youths and up to a dark and pregnant sky, and huddling within himself beneath a thick coat, embracing his crapulence like a cold familiar friend, with no degree of denial about what he is going to do.

Then along and up the winding paths beneath a canopy of bush, past the familiar lonesome forms on benches, and briefly out into a pool of yellow light before darkness once again. Richard's mind a mess of alcohol, and stoned; a few painkillers chucked in on top, though not enough for suicide – just to numb the pain. Looking at the rabbits as they hop unperturbed around the banks of grass beside the path – *'I feel like I'm in fucking Teletubby Land'* – laughing insanely to himself and wondering if anyone heard. Then up into the temple area; a few men standing around – *'I guess it's early yet, it is Saturday after all'* – and noticing a drizzling rain as he exits the temple and finds himself a lonely bench to sit on and gaze across at the whipped-up waves.

"Alright?" The depth of Richard's sedation is such that he has not registered someone sitting beside him. *"...Looks like a storm is coming. There's a place I know that's sheltered and out of the way ...if you're interested?"* Looking at the man, Richard is only able to make out his silhouette. His voice sounds all right, though – not too old or effeminate, and he can tell from his outline that he has a good build – *"Yeah... why not?"* – Richard's voice detached and monotone; as detached as his emotions as he follows the man down the bank

100

towards the skatepark, swept along by the bitter prevailing wind; over a fence and down past walls adorned with bright and complex graffiti to a rusted iron gate that hangs lopsided from a doorway. Then standing in the darkness and hearing the man fumble with a lighter in the dark before filling the room with the flickering of candlelight.

Looking around at the space in which he is standing, Richard is unsure as to its purpose. It is a concrete room with the remnants of some unidentifiable industrial machinery to one side. Part of the ceiling has a lower wooden alcove, which is blackened and half reduced to charcoal. The floor is covered with broken glass, rotting cardboard and empty three-litre bottles of cheap cider. In the corner, underneath the burned-out roof of the alcove, is a nest of cardboard, a torn and dirty foam mattress and some soiled sleeping bags and sheets. Looking at the man, Richard finds him handsome but with a wasted look – straining taut muscles that look as if they are about to burst through his skin, but are defined by a sunken surround, achieving a look of simultaneous strength and decay. He is cutting up some white powder. *"What's that?"* – Richard perking up a little at the prospect of drugs. *"Just some K ...good with fisting"* – looking at Richard with a twinkle in his eye. Richard warming to the imminent degradation – *"I've almost taken a fist ...can't get it in past the knuckles though"* – taking a seat on the mattress next to the man. *"...It takes practice, and training ...this'll help"* – the man meticulously straightening the two large lines – *"ahh, ketamine and fisting, the two perfect things to end an evening! ...I guess it's still a bit early, but never mind..."* – then becoming animated as something pops into his head – *"...it's like cheeses! ...Once you've tasted a really rotten Roquefort, you are not likely to appreciate the subtleties of an Edam, for instance..."* – becoming increasingly excited as his monologue takes form –

"it's always the mild cheeses first – most kids will only eat Dairylea ...then you progress to perhaps a mild cheddar, a sly wank, a glass of wine ...whatever; before you know it you're practically mainlining Gorgonzola! ...I like it hard myself ...hard sex, hard drugs ...hard cheese! HAHAHA ...fuckit, you only live once! ...I've got small hands as well, if you're up for it?" Richard looking at him blankly, confused by his cheese tangent. *"...Fisting?"* Richard registering as he goes to snort his line – *"oh ...yeah, whatever"* – the line burning Richard's nasal cavity, and feeling bunged up as the guy goes for his line; then Richard ... laying ... d-o-w-n ......the ... guy ... undoing ... his ... belt ... d-e-t-a-c-h-m-e-n-t ... *"... Lie ... on ... your ... front"*... mucus ... like ... cotton ... wool ... easing – in ... *"...that's ... it"* ... s-t-r-e-t-c-h ... a ... little ... more ... dimensions ... shifting ... *'Need – tissue...'* ...gag... swallowing ... bitter ... *"I ... like ... it ... rough"*... *"Oh ... yeah?"* ... *"B-o-n-d-a-g-e"*... withdrawal ... rummaging ... wrists ... bound ... rag ... in ... mouth ... dirt ... taste ... arse – up ... lube ... and ... s-t-r-e-t-c-h ... discomfort ... poppers ... *'Too ... much'* – too ... muffled ... s-t-r-e-t-c-h ... and ... biting ... in ... pain ... *"You ... can ... take ... it"* ... a-g-o-n-y ...and ... biting ... down ... on ... the ... pain ... *"push ... back ... on ... it ... it's ... nearly ... in"* ... – streaming ... eyes – ... *"that's ... it ... there's ... a ... good ... boy"* ... lost ... to ... the ... limits ... of ... sensation ... melting ... white ... nothingness ... *'And ... there ... is ... no ... redemption ... without ... sin'* ... lost ... in ... static ... *'and ... there ... is ...'* ... dissolve ... to ... white ... *"It's in, good boy ..."* ....

.... *"AAUUGH!"* – ridding his mouth of the rag and grit and coming to with a sudden acute awareness of his discomfort and degradation – *"...STOP ...stop, that's enough!"* The man surprised at first at the sudden outburst, then –

observing the genuine look of abject misery on Richard's face – obligingly withdrawing his fist and untying him – *"...I'm sorry – I thought you liked it rough..."* And Richard wiping the lube from his sore and stretched arsehole, then pulling up his trousers and putting on his coat, suddenly aware of the cold – *"...I guess I'm just in the wrong frame of mind ...sorry"* – then brushing down his clothes before heading out into icy and blistering rain, his movements still slow and detached, and back up the bank to the temple, to shelter for a moment and regain his composure.

Looking over into one of the adjacent chambers Richard can vaguely make out a group of about five or six figures, half masked by shadows. As he moves closer he can see the form of a guy in the centre of the group, legs splayed against the wall with his arse exposed; the men surrounding him are stroking their erections, and a couple have condoms already in place, ready to fuck. Richard looks on with a cold detachment as the first guy takes a stab. Guy 1's dick is too small and he can't keep it hard – it keeps slipping out, leaving the condom hanging from the fuckee's arse. Guy 2 is impatient – he pushes Guy 1 aside, shoving his unsheathed syphilitic cock inside and ramming hard, grating the guy's face against the wall as he penetrates; he comes in thirty seconds flat, impregnating the fuckee with a potpourri of STDs. Richard looking on, distant and emotionless; a feeling of repulsion crawls beneath his skin like scabies – *'Maybe it is ...I have been scratching a lot'* – Richard can make out some of the faces of the surrounding men. Some have lines etched deep into their leathery cheeks, others are not so old, but none seems particularly attractive. He can't make out much of the fuckee, who is too shrouded in shadows. A third guy reaches to pull the fuckee's head towards his cock... the fuckee stumbles – evidently drunk and quite oblivious; as he puts his hand out to break his fall it lands in a rectangle of light on the wall; Richard sees the ring.

It doesn't register fully at first – too wasted …just something familiar about that ring …that hand …Then slowly, seeping through his cold and distant shell, as the realisation twists deep inside and the emotions build; trying to break through the thick-skinned exterior Richard has developed. Richard wanting to reach out and grab Cameron, but as the pain and sadness wells all he can do is run and run from that place, run through the pouring rain, the filth of used condoms and mud swamped up from the flooding banks of soil and run, the bitter wind blistering his face and hands and run, his tendons pulling at the back of his calves and run, until tripping, stumbling, sprained and slumped exhausted under the seafront archways, the tears streaming from his face – *'…and there is no redemption…'* – tears for Cameron, for himself, for his mother – *"…Oh mother, look at me now…"* – *'…Without sin'* – *"…Your son – wouldn't you be proud"* – and laughing – *"look what I've accomplished …I can take a fist HAHAHA"* – and slapping at his head and running his fingers down until they run red furrows through the skin of his face and screaming and pulling at his hair and clenching his teeth into the flesh of his cheek, reopening old scar tissue… *'And there is no redemption…'*

For Alex, Salena and Ben

In memory of Phil and Fred

Thanks to Open Door, Jane and Ben Sumner, D and Han Neech, the Stapleton-Hibberts, Frankie Marino at Morpho's Lair, Rakewell, my parents and all who made this possible, especially Matilda – my medicine.

It is nothing: I am here; I am still here.
—Rimbaud

Portrait by Camilla Stapleton-Hibbert

Fearing imminent death after a positive HIV diagnosis, Oliver Speer / Spleen set to work to release his first proper collection of poetry and prose – within a year he had been hospitalised.

During his hospitalisation, the collection – titled "A Necrophiliac's Quiche" – gained notoriety, and plans were made for a film adaptation of his short story "Geoffrey's Numb".

Having survived, among other things, tuberculosis and a heart operation, Oliver found himself back in Hastings, the town of his birth – infamous in the late nineties as the drug, murder and suicide capital of the south. Here he began work on what was to become his first short novel, as well as playing the character Geoffrey in director Dickon Neech's twelve minute screen adaptation.

"Geoffrey's Numb" has been screened in venues ranging from the Ritzy in Brixton to Brighton's Cinematheque and the Odeon in Oliver's home town. It has been hailed by critics as "demented and sick" but with a "childlike quality", and "on a par with the student films of David Lynch".

"Depravikazi" is his first novel.